HEINZ HELLE was born in 1978. He studied philosophy in Munich and New York. He has worked as copywriter for advertising agencies, and is a graduate of the Swiss Literature Institute in Biel. *Superabundance* is his first book.

Praise for *Superabundance*

'*Superabundance* is a work of deadpan brilliance. The narrator's intellectual Tourette's becomes an exercise in unflinching honesty, chasing down lines of thought normally lost in the cacophony of our daily lives. I had always assumed I was fully conscious until I read this' Alex Christofi, author of *Glass*

'Helle writes in razor-sharp prose about existence in all its uncertainty' *Süddeutsche Zeitung*

'A compelling, nearly flawless story of total alienation' *Die Zeit*

'So modern, so cool, so strange' Hubert Winkels

'An enigmatic, clever and linguistically powerful piece of literature' Daniela Strigl

SUPERABUNDANCE

HEINZ HELLE

Translated by Kári Driscoll

With the support of the Swiss Arts Council Pro Helvetia

A complete catalogue record for this book can be obtained from the British Library on request

First published as *Der beruhigende Klang von explodierendem Kerosin* in 2014 by Suhrkamp Verlag, Berlin

First published in the UK in 2016 by Serpent's Tail,
an imprint of Profile Books Ltd
3 Holford Yard
Bevin Way
London
WC1X 9HD
www.serpentstail.com

ISBN 978 1 78125 395 3
eISBN 978 1 78283 129 7

Designed and typeset by sue@lambledesign.demon.co.uk
Printed and bound by CPI Group (UK) Ltd, Croydon, CR0 4YY

10 9 8 7 6 5 4 3 2 1

FSC
www.fsc.org
MIX
Paper from
responsible sources
FSC® C018072

SUPERABUNDANCE

He is still just a boy

You ask yourself what it's all about, and then you remember: the preservation of the species. The pitch is small, the grass dry and patchy, the lines are bare earth, not chalk, and beyond them just a single row of benches. The pitch is somewhere out in the suburbs. The corner flags are yellow, they're yellow everywhere, and beside the entrance to the clubhouse hangs the insignia of some obscure brewery. They're coming out, they're running up the basement steps in their blue-and-yellow and their green-and-white jerseys, the boys, they're eight or nine years old, and you watch them because you like it when members of a species have something that matters to them, when there is something in their lives to fight for, without weapons or violence. You're standing near the midfield line, right where they will run onto the field, and you clap your hands and are happy. One of them gives you a smile.

He is still just a boy. He is in goal. It's the first time he has been in goal, and he is thinking, all right, if you want me to be in goal, I'll be in goal, I don't mind. At first nothing happens. And when at some point a green-and-white striker comes running towards him, alone with the ball, he thinks nothing of it. The green-and-white striker doesn't shoot but gets closer and closer, and then suddenly the boy thinks, shit, I've got to make the save, and he thinks, I will make this save, because I'm doing all right, my parents are here as well, they've come just to see me play, and we even went and got twenty Chicken McNuggets at McDonald's beforehand, which I'll get at half time with sweet-and-sour sauce. But why have they put me in goal today? I'm really a defender, and a good defender at that, I'm probably a good goalie too, but how would they know that? I've never been in goal in my entire life, not even in training. I always get shouted at for ducking underneath the crosses, but this time I'm not scared, this time I won't duck. Here comes the green-and-white jersey, calm as you like. C'mon mate, take the shot will you? I'm not scared, so come on, show me what you've got. And suddenly he thinks that maybe he only *thinks* he's not scared, that he only *thinks* he'll make the save, that he only *thinks* he's a good goalie, and at that moment the green-and-white striker casually shoots the ball into the far corner, and the boy hurls himself after it because even though he hasn't got the slightest hint of a chance of reaching the ball, he doesn't want it to look like he's chicken. The match ends eight–nil.

I LEAVE

Is that something you can arrange?

Blanketing everything, the reassuring sound of exploding jet fuel. Greenland is grey. How much orange juice can you fit in an Airbus A340? The air hostesses' attractiveness must be proportionate to the distance from the earth at which they serve. To the suppressed proximity of death. Air and laughter made of plastic.

When we said goodbye, a warm breeze was blowing out of the tunnel. I pull the plastic film off the plastic chicken. It'll all work out, she said. And something else, but I only saw her mouth open, behind her the train thundered into the light, and then she closed her mouth again. Doors opened, people streamed past us, and I knew that she was not going to repeat it. As the aeroplane turned onto the runway, I asked myself why I was leaving. I asked myself why I was leaving when the engines began to roar and I was pressed into my seat and it took every ounce of will not to imagine a giant fireball and smouldering bodies and rescue personnel staring at blackened faces with no noses and exposed black teeth, in silence, in the snow. I know exactly why I am leaving. It's getting dark.

A beer would be nice.

Perhaps one day they will figure out what it means to be *here* and to see *this* and feel *that*. What it means to be 'me'. They will discover a specific neuronal pattern that is so unique in its complexity and frequency, so divine, so incredibly beautiful, that the explication of its structure will automatically explain its content. Then they will say: we know what consciousness is. And then they will be able to synthesise it. They will finally have gained control over the 'I'. Then I will go to them and say: I mustn't ever stop loving her, ever. Is that something you can arrange?

The hot cloth on my face is already almost cold. I return my seat and tray table to their upright positions. We begin our descent into New York. The false calm during controlled falling. I know that nothing really explodes inside a jet engine. Then lights outside windows that I'm not sitting at, and waiting and falling and waiting and falling and a loud, salvific thud. I have absolutely no fear of flying, I think, as we roll along the runway. I remain seated with my seat belt fastened until we are parked at the gate. Outside my window, well lit, empty stretches of tarmac. Maybe it was a mistake to leave. But this is the only brain I've got.

I try not to think about her

So I am on my way. I am leaving an airport building. I am carrying a suitcase and the suitcase is heavy. Out of a black sky fall dots of white. In front of me taxis, behind me an arrivals hall, inside which there are wet-gleaming linoleum floors in lighter shades of grey, upon which there are people, luggage, red, yellow, black or brown vending machines and metallic seating with imitation leather upholstery, automatic glass doors, automatic glass doors opening, people arriving, people picking up, customs, the baggage carousel, many more baggage carousels, passport control, the queue for passport control, corridors, banners, information and signs displaying prohibited items, escalators, stairs, a corridor, a corridor inside an arm between the airport and the plane, an arm they call the jet bridge, an aeroplane, the Atlantic Ocean. And her.

I fall into the soft upholstery of a taxi's back seat, I say an address, I try not to notice that the driver's skin is a different colour from mine, try, having taken out the agreed-upon 60 dollars, not to put my wallet away as quickly as possible just because the driver's skin is a different colour from mine. On the radio there are voices speaking English and I recognise the music but it still sounds strange, at this particular moment, in this particular place. The white dots falling out of the black sky grow larger and more numerous, the lights more yellow and irregular, the asphalt in the cone of the headlights grows lighter and broader, receding faster and faster underneath me. It goes up, down, up, viaducts, entry ramps, exit ramps, the lines are yellow and dotted, tyres thud in the cracks between slabs of concrete, and at some point the blackness of the sky is overlaid with a different blackness, shadows, even though there is no sun, of buildings, larger and more of them than I have ever seen before, and then we crash onto one of those famous bridges and into a tangle of steel, light and cars, and the lights are red, blue and green and I think I really should be overwhelmed by these first incredible impressions of this incredible city and I think probably this is what it feels like to be overwhelmed by the first incredible impressions of this incredible city and so I get my phone out of my bag and type a message to her that says: incredible.

I arrive at an old industrial building. This is the address I gave the driver. I give him money and get out of the taxi. Under the doormat there's a key. The elevator smells like hydraulic fluid. I get out on the fifth floor. The apartment is small and unheated. I put my suitcase down, rummage around in it for warm clothes that I can wear over the ones I'm already wearing, then I leave the apartment, the elevator, the building, walk along broad sidewalks past dark, deserted warehouses until I am walking past dark, shuttered display windows, until at a crossing one is illuminated and I squeeze underneath the half-closed shutter past the tightly spaced shelves filled with oversized packaging and get bread, crisps, beer and a newspaper. I pay and leave the deli, which even now is not closing. I leave behind loud voices at the check-out; the owner and two customers are having an argument, I'm not sure if it's between them or with the world, with suppliers, tax inspectors or wives. I think they're speaking Polish.

I return to the former industrial building. I lie down in the short bed under the thin sheets and I drape over them articles of clothing that aren't much thicker. I eat the bread and the crisps and drink the beer and stare at the letters printed on the newspaper and I lie awake for a long time, maybe because in the place where I woke up this morning it's already light. It's dark enough to sleep and I don't know if I can't because it's so early or because it's so cold. Every now and then I look through the small window across the flat roofs between my building and the river towards the towers of light on the other side. Somewhere over there is where I'll go tomorrow and see where I'll be working and I don't feel annoyed or upset or anything. I have no opinion about my inability to sleep, and I ask myself whether I shouldn't have an opinion about it or if not about that then at least whether I should have an opinion about something else, and if so then what, and then I ask myself what she would do in this situation and of course that doesn't make it any better, and so I try not to think about her, which of course makes me think about her even more, dammit, and then thank God it's maybe not exactly day, but the sky is growing lighter. And I get out of bed and out of the room and out of the building, and walk with dulled steps as if over plastic sheeting to the subway station through my steaming breath. The cars are frosted over.

I look around sometimes

I am sitting at a desk. It is a desk like any other. Around me, other people are sitting at other desks, and each of us has been allotted tasks, for the completion of which we are given something we can exchange for food, clothing and shelter. Our task is to find solutions to problems. Our tasks differ only according to the problems that need solving. In front of me there is a computer. Next to me sit people, and in front of them there are computers too. Someone is also sitting across from me. Occasionally we write, occasionally we read, then we write some more. We do not speak. What we write is influenced by what we read. What we read has been written by people who either have more power and influence than we do, or less. If they have more power, it must be considered more carefully. If they don't, it won't be. What we write will be read by people who either have more power and influence than we do or less. The powerful can force us to write it all over again. We don't care about those less powerful than us. For the most part we write what is expected of us.

I am sitting at a desk. Behind me is a wall of glass. Behind that a street, snowdrifts, fast people and slow cars, in front of me the empty white page of the word-processing program. Then, letters, words, a sentence on the white page of the word-processing program, and the sentence has something to do with the problem that I am trying to solve. I look at the sentence carefully. Word by word, character by character. Then I press a key and the sentence disappears, dissolves into the white of the page. I know that today is Tuesday and that soon I have to give a lecture about the problems I am dealing with, and that I am supposed to outline some solutions I find promising. I also know that it is important that I describe the problems in a way such as only I can describe them, that I outline solutions that only I can outline, otherwise what I am doing could just as easily be done by someone else. I know all of this, but I do nothing. I stare at my screen and do nothing. The cursor on the white page of the word-processing program blinks steadily, slow and thin.

I look around sometimes. I see a woman sitting two rows behind me who has dark hair and a silver earring and she senses that I'm looking at her, and she looks at me too, and then we both look away. I stare a little longer at my screen and out of the window, I see wall, street, snow, cars, I look back at her, she looks at me. I wonder if she's simply reacting to the presence of a member of the opposite sex in her field of vision, as evolution instructs her to do. I wonder if, having carefully evaluated my phenotypical characteristics, she would be interested in a transfer of some of my genetic material, or if she has discovered something about me, something fascinating, beautiful, special or repugnant, evil, sad, something that she can't put into words and for which she has no evidence, but that she is certain is there, and although she finds it uncomfortable to look at me every time I look at her, and she gets chills down her spine from arousal or disgust, she simply can't look away, because I am exactly the way I am.

I am staring at my screen and thinking that really I know full well that what I'm thinking is nonsense and I ask myself why I am thinking it. And then I think that sooner or later it had to come to this, that here I am once again thinking about whether the fact that I am thinking about a random woman means that she and I no longer have a chance, that I don't really want her anymore, without knowing it, or can't want her, or don't want to be able to want her, and it seems to me that wanting isn't something you can control, no matter how hard you try. I don't know if there's some drug to prevent the blurring of levels of meaning, and I also don't know whether my problem has to do with the blurring of levels of meaning, by which I don't mean the problem that's been assigned to me here at my desk. No, I mean my personal problem. If there were some drug for what I've got, whatever it is, I would want it.

There is a problem with your insurance

I step into the staff-manager's office. Her name is Rita and she will be ready for me in a few minutes. I take a seat in an imitation leather armchair wedged into a partitioned office cubicle. Women of every weight and race sit working in the other cubicles. I cross my legs, and Rita calls me in.

Hello.

Hello. There is a problem with your insurance.

I don't know what problem that could be, all I know is that I have got insurance, so I don't say anything, but only look at her wide-eyed, though not too wide-eyed. I don't want to seem impolite or sceptical or arrogant.

There is nothing in your contract about who pays for the cost of shipping your body to Germany.

I don't understand.

If – God forbid – you died over here.

I know that my insurance policy says that it covers one hundred per cent of all costs, so I say so.

But it says in my certificate that one hundred per cent of costs are covered.

Yes, I saw that. But it doesn't say who will pay for the shipping of your remains to Germany.

But isn't that included in one hundred per cent?

It doesn't say so.

I'm sure it is included.

I'm afraid that isn't enough. I will need your insurance company to confirm that.

I nod. I get up. I shake her hand. I see her perfect white teeth, through which she utters an astonishingly loud apology for the trouble, or a thank you for your cooperation, or a stop being such an idiot. I don't know. I'm not listening. I am trying to work out whether the people at my insurance company in Germany are still at work, so that I can ask them if they can confirm in writing that they will cover the cost of repatriating my body, even if I'm no longer inside it or at least am no longer aware that I'm inside it, since presumably I am it. My body, that is.

I don't want to take the lift, so I press the big shiny bar that opens the door into the stairwell. I see steps. I step on the first step. It is made of concrete. It goes clong. The edge is reinforced with a steel strip. I step on the second, third, fourth steps. They also go clong. I step on the fifth, sixth, seventh steps. The walls are painted yellow.

I step onto the landing, it goes tock. The concrete here is naked and dull. And then it goes clonk, clonk again. More yellow walls, and the light is artificial but pleasantly unobtrusive. I reach the sixth floor, the fifth, fourth, third, second, and suddenly it goes calong. One of the steel strips is loose. Presumably, a bolt has come undone and rolled, then fallen into the basement, where it was presumably swept up and disposed of along with chewing-gum wrappers, pebbles, dirt and dust, and presumably it is now lying in a larger heap of chewing-gum wrappers, pebbles, dirt and dust, and other remnants of rust, which no longer belong to any one specific bolt, and where it will gradually decompose and decompose, until it is fine, hard, special dust among dust.

I open the door to the street. I jump off the last step of the building, and now I am floating, and at that precise moment my form, comprised of deoxyribonucleic acid sequences, my ability to remember various moments from my childhood and various things learnt at school, the feelings I once had or have repressed or forgotten, the people who have influenced or harmed or coddled me, and all the possibilities from the merger of one of my father's spermatozoa and one of my mother's egg cells that became a reality 9,964.5 days ago in this single, semi-permeable object, vaguely separated from the mixture of gases that surround it, hits the concrete slab of pavement and the only repercussion it has on the world are tiny vibrations on the surface of a puddle of oil in the gutter, far below the threshold of my perception.

I ask myself whether I'm on the right path

I'm drinking beer. I'm sitting at a café near my office. It smells of grease and drying coats. The café is really more of a self-service restaurant. It is astonishingly large, the room is just ten metres wide but fifty metres deep, it just keeps going further and further back towards a staircase leading up to a second level, a colourful, brightly lit rectangle beneath the mountains of concrete at the edge of the street. I walk along the pizza counter, the salad bar, past the sushi buffet and the pots of soup, I stop by the roast beef, take some along with some rice and, because it's healthy, some broccoli. I don't touch it. The amount of meat I throw away a few minutes later only briefly makes me feel guilty. It didn't taste good, and that piece of dead animal that's going into the rubbish isn't any deader just because it's in the rubbish.

I ask myself whether I'm on the right path towards solving the problem I've been tasked with or not. I don't have an opinion on the matter. I don't know if that makes me feel disappointed or angry or if I basically don't care. I don't know if it's bad that I don't know how I feel about the progress of my work. I don't know if someone else in my position would know how they felt about it, or would have an impulse, a need to do something or not to do something, to take a decision to make a change, or not make a change and just keep following the path that has led him to this place, steadfast, direct, inexorable. One thing I know for certain: she would know what to do.

Then a child screams. It's the kind of scream that expresses neither pain nor sorrow, but profound rage. A scream like a dial tone, only two octaves higher. His mother alternates between offering the boy lying face-down on the floor a chocolate bar and his plastic fire engine, but this does nothing to alter his composure or his volume. I sense how sustained screaming causes my neutral-to-benevolent stance towards not-yet-fully-grown people to switch. From one moment to the next I am filled with antipathy and disgust, which doesn't play out in my stomach but in my head. I, too, want to scream. Before I can give this more serious consideration, the mother suddenly grows loud as well. The boy screams again, his scream is so high-pitched that inwardly I call him a queer, which is ridiculous, since for one thing he's not even sexually mature yet and so has no sexual preferences, and for another a person's sexual preferences have nothing whatsoever to do with the pitch of their voice. He goes on screaming.

The mother stamps her foot. If I were her son, I would laugh out loud at this point. My body gets up off the chair – slap him – my knees stretch, the chair slides backward – come on you spineless bitch, a slap in the face never hurt anyone – I see a hand imprinted on the boy's cheek, not permanently, just for a moment, and I see clearly how the soft tissue below his eye shifts towards his nose the moment that large adult hand strikes it. It's a man's hand. I straighten my spine. It hurts. I spend too much time sitting these days. I've been telling myself that for five years now. I sidle out of the space between table and chair and make an effort not to look in the boy's direction. He shouldn't suspect, not yet. My legs move in the direction of the rubbish bin. What is left on the tray, napkins and an empty beer bottle, fall into it. I turn and find myself heading straight for the boy, feel the gravitational pull between my hand and his face. In six steps I'll have reached him, four, three, two. The mother bends down and picks his wriggling body up, kisses him on the cheek and silences his screams with her infinitely patient right ear. It is not until I'm out on the street, as tiny ice crystals strike my eyes through the slits into which I have narrowed my eyelids, that I realise I haven't slapped him.

The cold feels good.

I stay a while longer

That evening, I'm with two famous philosophers at a
Japanese restaurant on 36th Street. Two famous philosophers and about thirty other professors, graduate
students and undergraduates. The food isn't arriving. We
order another round of sake. The famous, plump functionalist and the slightly less famous, less plump representationalist are talking about God. The guy sitting next
to me is telling me about an article he read recently about
Germany, which he found quite interesting, and which he
promises to bring along to the next session of our interdisciplinary seminar on consciousness and neuroscience.
Thank God. The sake arrives, it's warm and smooth, my
neighbour's fiancée arrives late, she'd had work to finish.
She's taller than he is and thinner and teaches something
at some college or other. They touch each other a lot and
kiss occasionally, they hold hands, and she says that
she is divorced. I don't say a word, but no one notices.
Our waiter tells us he is Korean, but no one would have
noticed that, either. At some point, our food arrives.
The functionalist and the representationalist are still

talking about God. I'm a little confused, since I thought they were both atheists. At any rate they are both fierce opponents of the possibility of a non-physically explainable element of consciousness, i.e. what used to be called the soul, and yet here they are talking about God, and not in the way you would talk about something that doesn't exist, or at least not really, like unicorns or square circles. The Spanish exchange student is criticising evolutionary theory, not on religious but on formal grounds. I try to listen, but my neighbour is telling me that the problem with Germany, according to the article on Germany he read, is the works councils.

What do I say to that? Well, you know, yes, I think the works councils do have too much power, I say, and I think, but don't say, that not even God would have the power to make square circles, whereas unicorns probably wouldn't be a problem. The functionalist and the representationalist are talking about God without asking the theodicy question, which makes sense, since for them evil doesn't exist, things are either evolutionarily functional or evolutionarily non-functional, some things represent, others are represented, that's it. God has nothing to do with it, and to them He has no business being part of a scientific theory.
But He's perfectly all right for personal use. I like God, the representationalist is saying. He is a very nice thing.

When the food arrives, my neighbour says that it's cool to be sitting in a Japanese restaurant having dinner with two famous philosophers. And they're talking about God, I say. Yes, he says, that's cool as well, even though he doesn't believe in Him, and what's my opinion on the matter? I don't want to say that I don't know, because I so often say that and because I have the feeling that my reality is composed of the things I say. So long as I only think things, they won't hurt anyone. So instead I say, I believe in works councils.

Laughter. I am mildly pleased with myself, I try to smile in a charming and modest way, but I have the feeling that people can see through it, so I smile a little more broadly, grin, try to look the same way I am feeling, and then I notice that I am perhaps grinning a little too broadly at my own joke, and so I quickly take a sip of sake, followed by a sip of beer. The laughter fades away before I can put the bottle back down.

No, really, my neighbour insists. I say, Well, you know, I don't think God has any business in a scientific theory either, repeating the words of the representationalist. A-ha, my neighbour nods, underwhelmed by this hedge, and then I stick my neck out with: But what science doesn't grasp, we can't say anything about. I am worried that this will initiate a discussion about epistemology and I try to decide whether I'm more of a realist or an antirealist today, but just then my neighbour's fiancée says she wants to go. Oh, too bad, all right, I'll bring you the newspaper with that article next week, great, see you, yes, get home safely, bye bye.

I stay a while longer, I always stay a while longer, until at some point everyone else has gone, or I'm too drunk to see the faces around me as familiar. Or perhaps it's the others who are too drunk. More rounds of sake are ordered, I order a beer as well, and then suddenly everybody gets up and throws their credit cards down in the middle, first the two famous philosophers, then the professor from New Jersey, then the Spanish exchange student, and finally me. I am the last, as if I had been trying to get out of paying. I am now wondering if the others are looking at me strangely, and so their looks inevitably seem strange to me, and I can't bring myself to take part in the negotiations about how to split the bill, so I pay whatever's left over, which is not much, and I've probably had more to drink than anyone else. Since I am already standing up and can tell that I won't be able to find a way back into the conversation, I cross the restaurant to get my coat. I put it on and walk back to the table, hoping that wearing my coat will absolve me of having to announce my decision to leave, but no one reacts, which is why I start shaking hands, at the end of the table furthest away from the famous philosophers. Oh, you're leaving? Too bad.

When I get to the famous philosophers, I shake the hand of the one whose guest I am officially. I mumble something which he presumably doesn't understand, and I don't understand what he mumbles back. The other famous philosopher is in the gents, or outside smoking, or else he's looking the other way. At any rate, I'm definitely not going to shake hands with him just because he's famous. I don't know him at all. As I head towards the exit, I can feel the eyes of the hard core of the interdisciplinary seminar on consciousness and neuroscience on my back. I can hear their thoughts about the credit card thrown down too late, about my obduracy interpreted as arrogance, or my arrogance interpreted as obduracy, and yet as I pass another thirty tables whose occupants I studiously avoid looking at, I can nevertheless clearly tell that absolutely no one is paying any attention to me.

What's your problem?

I think my language centre is more robust than my sense of balance. With my right hand I place the shot glass on the bar, which I'm no longer simply leaning on with my left hand, but clinging to, and say, Same again please. Music. To my left, the loud, popular professor from New Jersey, from that university no one's heard of. To my right, the farmer's son from Alabama who wanted to become a priest but remained a student. We chat a little about our problems, not because we lose sleep over them but because it is our job to have problems. We're all in the same job, which is why it's OK for us to be imbibing nerve toxins together like this. Who else would you do that with, other than with friends maybe?

I can see the big mouth of the professor from that university in New Jersey that no one has heard of, it is opening and closing, opening and closing, his cheeks tremble when he laughs, because he thinks he is right or has had a good idea. I like the fact that he feels the need to talk to me about my problems, that he believes that he is interested in what I have to tell him. I like the fact that he is so completely convinced of the need to have an opinion about me and about everything that anyone might say that he doesn't even notice that he's got an opinion, he just has.

He quotes, illuminates new aspects, analyses, interprets, questions, criticises, and I want to say, Shut up you wanker I love you same again please. What?

Same again, please.

The farmer's son joins us in the next round of shots, in more illuminating, more questioning, more understanding. More maybe this is what you meant? Is that not what you meant? That wouldn't be a bad idea.

You think that would be a good idea?

Yes.

Yes.

Then probably that's what I meant.

My unwillingness to hide my own opportunism provokes an awkward silence, or maybe it's the shots, or maybe it's not an awkward silence but rather an understanding one, sympathy for my honesty perhaps, or compassion for my despair, or that feeling you sometimes get when you're drinking with people you don't know at all, the feeling of knowing how they're feeling because you yourself feel so and so, and feelings really are a complicated matter, and truth and all that, and you know what I mean?

Yes.

Yes.

I can't tell if their smiles are genuine, it's too dark. I can't tell if mine is genuine, too much alcohol, but at this moment the three of us are the best friends in the whole world, our backs bent over the bar at similar angles, parallel lines on the path to infinity, we hearseethink and drink here side by side.

And love, of course, and what the hell does that arsehole think he's looking at? I clutch my glass more tightly, if I need to smash it in his face the part I'm holding onto should remain intact, and the music goes bam bam.

After a while we're discussing the question of whether or not we'll ever be able to find answers. Whether it's possible, not to prove a system on the basis of itself, that's impossible as we know, as such and such has already shown, but whether it's still possible to perceive it, recognise it, love it. The music goes bam bam, and that arsehole is still looking at us, and we return to the things we were talking about before. They use words I can't define, and I answer with words I can't define, but apparently don't use entirely incorrectly. They look to see if I have something more to say, or if I've already said everything. I look to see if that arsehole is still looking. He is looking. I squeeze my glass. You're empty, says the loud professor from the university in New Jersey that no one's heard of. Same again, please.

Yes.

Yes.

I ask myself whether I would be able to define the word Yes, and what there really is to say about Yes apart from when to use it in a sentence, and even that is hard enough.

Do you like New York?

Yes.

We drink, and at some point I reach that moment, it happens, something changes, something inside seeps out, goes away, and the person who's left behind says what he says, stands the way he stands, and moves the leg that's resting on the metal rod underneath the bar tentatively in time to the music. It is good. The things around me have stopped screaming out their names, what there is just is, just like that. The bar's smooth, shiny wood, the professor's pot belly, the ladies' clothes, the thin band of dark yellow light over the black floor and the white wall, the dancers' arms in the air above them, their smell, their laughter, a bam, another bam, and the arsehole who is still staring, what's your problem?

My problem is the question of why we experience anything. My problem is the question of why our bodies, with their intricate perceptive and processing apparatus, in addition to all that perception and processing, also produce something like an oh, so this is what it's like to be me and here and now and doing this specific thing, or not. My problem is the question of what a scientific theory to explain our consciousness would have to look like. My problem is the fact that it sounds cool to say I'm a philosopher so I study philosophy. My problem is that I'm drunk and I want to fuck, but I'm a philosopher and so really problems like consciousness and experience should be more important to me than women. My problem is that I love a woman but I think that I will at some point stop loving her and I renounce a world in which that is possible. My problem is that I am a philosopher and I work on consciousness, i.e. what we used to call the soul, and I am sometimes afraid that the others who say that consciousness is nothing but an illusion might be right, because if they are then when we die we just die. My problem is that I'm a philosopher and so I sometimes think that if p is any given phenomenal truth and q is the conjunction of all physical facts, then p cannot be deduced from q.

I don't have a problem, I say to the arsehole, who at that moment is not staring any more, and there is no more hatred in his eyes, no interest, no anger, he's just not staring any more, never was staring at me, just at the spot where I happen to be standing, because he's staring where he's staring and he doesn't care who or what might be occupying that space. His gaze is not the kind one can move into or out of, his gaze falls out of him and on the world, and he alone steers it, and to him I don't even exist. I let go of my glass.

She who is not her

I have no idea what time it is. Someone is lying beside me. It's not her. My head is not my head. She who is not her is actually quite pretty. I'm still drunk. She who is not her is still here. I pull away the covers. She who is not her is still quite pretty. A furrow on her brow, a deep, uncompromising sleep that is forcing the alcohol out of her bloodstream and the last traces of laughter out of her face. I look at her breasts. My hand reaches between her legs and I don't find it strange or disgusting or arousing, I don't find it anything. But that wall back there, I've seen that before, I know the guy who lives here, and I didn't think he was the type of guy who did this type of thing. She who is not her is badly shaved, and I've still got a hard-on. She who is not her is scratchier than my chin. She who is not her does not wake up and as I slip on the condom I am reminded of a picture I saw at a restaurant once of Indians with buffalo heads sneaking up on a grazing herd. She who is not her still does not wake up. He who really doesn't do this sort of thing carries on. Really, it's already too light for this sort of thing. I close my eyes.

I see myself the night before, when it's still dark. It's about midnight, and at first my head is not my head. Let's play a game, says a she who is also not her. We'll each come up with a false identity and then we'll each go talk to five strangers and afterwards we'll tell each other what happened. It's perfect for parties where you don't know anyone, says she who is also not her.

After all, we don't know each other. Which is why we're having this stupid conversation about this strange game played by two idiots who don't know anyone. Who both end up standing around on their own and eventually find one another. Like in PE at school when you're the last to be picked. For the moment I am still telling myself that I could strike up a conversation with anyone at this party any time if I wanted to. But I don't want to. Why did she who is also not her decide to speak to me anyway? She's got short hair. She's actually got quite a pretty face.

Or soap bubbles?

What?

It would be fun to blow soap bubbles, says she who is also not her, shooting a glance at the packet of cigarettes I have just taken out of my pocket.

I don't smoke, you see, says she who is also not her. Which is a shame. If you smoke you can go outside and be outside and talk outside, but if you don't smoke you just stand around outside without anything to do, which is why it would be fun to blow soap bubbles, says she who is also not her.

I put the cigarettes back in my pocket and take a sip of gin. Does she who is also not her take my silence as a sign of agreement or of indifference? Would agreement be off-putting or encouraging, or would she who is also not her try even harder the more indifferent I was? She really does have quite a pretty face, but that short hair.

What are you doing in New York?

I'm a visiting scholar at the City University.

What department?

Philosophy.

Really? You teach philosophy?

No, I'm working on a paper, I say, and I don't think my tone of voice has changed and yet she who is also not her takes a step closer to me and says, with a serious look on her face: I won't ask you what it's about.

Thanks, I say, and for the first time in our conversation I laugh.

Very kind of you, I say, and she who is also not her begins to laugh as well, and this would be the beginning of something that could have come to a relaxed, conciliatory end for two egos and at the least my libido in my bed or in hers, if only she who is also not her didn't have such short hair.

I see myself when it's a little darker still, probably around three, and I see myself walking into an apartment in the financial district with someone else who is likewise not her and who has a spectacular cleavage and long blonde hair and suddenly begins to cry uncontrollably because apparently she who is likewise not her has acne – I can't see that clearly by this point – and while she who is likewise not her is in the bathroom blowing her nose and drying her eyes, I realise that I am only here to see past her acne and to prove to her that it is possible for someone to find her beautiful and to prove to myself that someone wants to be found beautiful by me. Otherwise there is no reason for my presence here. And so I take off the T-shirt with the amusing cartoon figure on it that she who is likewise not her has given me to sleep in and leave the apartment. In the hallway I look briefly out of the window. I've never been so high up in New York before. The doorman does not seem surprised when I go past him for the second time in the space of twenty minutes.

I see myself when it's so dark that I can't quite see who is sitting next to me in the taxi taking us back to Brooklyn, but I assume it's the person lying next to me right now, she who is not her. The taxi driver taking us to Brooklyn asks me if I'm from Germany and talks to me at first about the Autobahn, then about Porsche, then about the Jews, and I'm relieved when we get out. I freely accept his business card. Call me and I'll send you a picture of my Mustang, he says, because he's got a Mustang, wouldn't that be something, him and his Mustang on the German Autobahn.

Through my closed eyelids I sense light. In my stomach something falls over. Hurriedly I get up and stumble into the bathroom. As my knees hit the tiles on either side of the toilet bowl I hear the front door close. I have no idea where she who is not her came from. But I know she isn't her. Before the gag reflex sets in, the saliva pools in my mouth.

Superabundance

I step into the kitchen. I think: I have to give a lecture soon. I don't think: coffee cup. Nevertheless, I open the right cupboard. The refrigerator reaches my shoulder and is louder than the cars outside the window. The fridge door is heavy, the milk cold. A short while later, something hot and brown is flowing into me, it would be an exaggeration to say that it tastes good, but in any case it has flavour, and my entire existence is reduced to the interplay of my senses of taste and smell, combined with tactile and temperature information from my oral cavity, electrical impulses to my brain. They don't ask why, they say: this is how it is.

I take a shower. I get dressed. I step out onto the street. The traces of alcohol in my bloodstream support me for a change, help me not to notice anyone but myself. In front is in front, right right, left left, and what's behind doesn't matter. Then, suddenly, this is in front of me, and then that is in front of me, and I feel a gentle gust of air against my eyes, moist from the cigarette smoke.

The bare walls and the parked cars are the only indication that I am moving forwards, the sky is thick and grey, the buildings are invisible. Air parts in front of my face, nitrogen molecules stream across the skin of my forehead, oxygen, carbon dioxide, methane. The air resistance seems to be increasing, no doubt clouds are moving across the grey sky up there, and no doubt they are heavy with something that I cannot at this moment sense, even though I know exactly what is coming. Then it begins, the falling. A snowflake, five, a thousand, millions, unperturbed, independently of me, they fall downward from above, while I fall horizontally through them.

I walk along Bedford Avenue. Melt water that has crept for hundreds of metres along steel trusses forms pools under the bridge, where, mixed with tiny particles of rust, it waits to evaporate. A group of Hispanics are hanging out on the corner. They too are waiting for something, though I have no idea what. On the side of the road there are old refrigerators, gas stoves, ovens, air conditioners, graffiti on the walls. I walk into a café. I order, nod, say Thank you. It's good when everything runs smoothly, it's good to have a role in the solar system, even if it only consists of ordering a burger, eating, paying, and then at some later point, defecating. As my fork pierces the last piece of bloody beef, I think bloody beef. Then I think about eyes and a bolt gun, and I ask myself why I can't just think: that was really tasty. The words in my head don't exist, I say to the words in my head.

I leave. I am standing at a crossing. On the street, people are moving in machines designed for transportation in various colours and shapes. Some of these machines send a message about the social status of the people sitting inside them, others do not. In not sending a message, they also send a message. There is noise. Lights. Solicitations to buy, enjoy, see a movie or attend an event, accept an ideal of beauty or a role in society. None of these solicitations has anything in common with the others, except for the fact that they are all solicitations. I am unable to discern any underlying structure behind all these codes. No method, no goal, together they are a swamp of emotions, convictions, duties and dreams. Images, words. Fog. Amidst the blackened slush a child's shoe. Taxis. The freedom of not having to do anything, the pressure of being able to do anything, the brutal, or, depending on one's mood and disposition, gentle, fact of the omnipresence of something or other. The unignorability of being alive.

When I get home, I sit at the kitchen table and try not to think about anything. It doesn't work. The more I concentrate on pushing words out of my consciousness, the harder they come crashing back, off the walls, the

furniture, the unopened letters in between the old news-
papers on the table, off the colour of the sky, the shape
of the clouds, the smell in the kitchen. And for a while
they fly around the room and then settle over the world.
Words suffocate everything innate, everything independent, they take as much Being as they can and turn it into
a My. My pen, my paper, my table, my breadcrumbs on
my table, my scraps of tobacco, my plastic wrapper in the
terracotta ashtray on the table next to the piece of paper,
my tree, inside which grew the sheet I am writing now,
my earth on which it stood, my saw, which cut it down,
my mine, from which the iron ore was extracted to make
the saw, and what's left is my nothing.

Now I am cocking the hammer, and now the cylinder turns,
now the barrel touches my cheekbone, and instantly the
pain in my head is gone, and I pull the trigger, and it digs
into my fingertip until the flesh between bone and steel
becomes firm enough to relay the pressure, and I don't
hear the explosion because it takes too long to travel
through my auditory canal to the parts of my ear responsible for reporting explosions or else because those parts
have already been penetrated by the smooth steel-jack-
eted bullet, destroying millions, billions of connections,
an image of myself as a young boy on the football pitch,
the first binomial formula and the words of the German
national anthem and the reason why it's only the third

verse, shalala, all gone. Grey matter sprayed wildly across the room. Or else because the steel has already reached that part of me usually in charge of projecting the illusion that there is a 'me' there for whom the illusion is being projected, before I can hear it coming, or else the gun isn't loaded, or I don't even own a gun, or even if I did I wouldn't have enough courage to pull the trigger, or I wouldn't have enough sorrow, rage, boredom, hate, or I'd have too much, which would stop me from pulling the trigger, in there, where there is no steel, only soft concepts rubbing up against each other like a crowd of people who only begin to panic because they know there's no way out.

I leave the apartment. I do not take the old industrial elevator that smells of hydraulic fluid. Instead, I take the stairs. Not down. Up. On the top floor it gets dark. The stairs get narrower, steeper, but they lead further up. I look up. I can't see anything. I take the steps one at a time till I reach the last one. I hold out my hand. My hand finds a wooden trap door. I can feel the rough wood, the cold. I push. Nothing. I push harder. Slowly the trap door gives way. A second dawn. It squeaks, stands, teeters, falls. I step outside. From the rooftop I can see a big, empty sky. Below it other roofs, with graffiti on them. Brilliant colours above the grey city. Flowers indifferent to the seasons and to the law proliferate upon the wild stone that grows at right angles in all directions. A super-abundance of surfaces.

I go back to my apartment. Outside the window the thick grey behind the tangle of steel over the river, light dissolving like the colours before it and the shapes in which people live, supposedly, and: snowflakes. A slowly solidifying screen over reality.
She's coming tomorrow.

WE ARE BEAUTIFUL

She comes and stands next to me

I am standing at the window. Condensation collects at the bottom edge of the windowpane. I see the river, see buildings where people live, doing things I can't see but which I can with some justification assume that they are doing, after all I too live in a building and do things such as, for example, standing at the window. I don't see anyone standing at any of the windows I can see, the sky is reflected in some of them, in others the concrete façade of an adjacent building, in others other windows. I am looking out of the window at a city that means everything to some people, a lot to many, nothing to none. I see a city, it's the city I currently live in, and the desires, motives and actions of the other people, whose existence in my field of vision I can only infer, are as abstract and distant as the forces keeping Jupiter's third moon in orbit. Like the condensation at the bottom of my windowpane, people gather in specific places for various reasons, clothed in differently tailored fabrics, with differently shaped pieces of rubber or leather to create a minimal distance between them and the celestial body they call home. All these people are surrounded by more or less the same mixture of gases, their skin receiving similar information about temperature and wind; in their stomachs similar substances are being dissolved, organic vegetable and animal matter. Many of them are feeling something, perhaps contentment, perhaps the hope of professional or personal success, of a fatty dinner, or sexual intercourse.

Then she comes and stands next to me and looks out of the window with me, and her smell and the smell of the cup of coffee in her hand are more real than the planet I am standing on. Her hand gently touches my hip and I feel the warmth and softness and plasticity of her body, as close to me as the laws of physics allow. The buildings and windows and the sky out there, the river, the streets, the bridges, the clouds, the helicopters, the people flying them, the subway trains beneath the earth's surface and the ones on the bridges, the neighbourhood directly opposite, and the one left of that, and the one on the right, the one behind me on the other side of the drywall and the hallway and the apartment opposite and the people in it and their furniture, clothes, hobbies and political convictions, all these things I can think of while looking around me suddenly acquire infinite mass and break loose of their moorings in the abstract and begin to fall, fast, faster, along the invisible and inexplicable line we call reference. They fall out of my head and back into the world when she says: Beautiful city. We are standing at the window.

We think of each other as friends

The first time we see each other, we're in a former army vehicle depot on the site of a former barracks. Now it's full of internet start-ups and print shops and the events agency at which we're both doing an internship because neither of us is quite sure what we want to do for a living. I'm twenty-four, she's twenty-one. She is wearing baggy, low-rise corduroys and she is bringing a form into the office where I am sitting and we say Hello and don't spare each other much of a second thought. I've got a girlfriend who's bipolar. She's got a boyfriend who's bisexual, as I soon discover, and evidently we're both doing well enough that we don't need each other.

We see each other again. At clubs, cafés, bars, always with other people. We greet each other warmly and talk. We begin to think of each other as friends. She's got a new boyfriend who's jealous and from East Germany. I'm still with my bipolar girlfriend, somehow. I'm drunk and strangely not thinking about sex as I sit down next to her, instead I tell her how it's not always easy to be in a relationship with someone who's bipolar and she tries to reassure me. I don't tell her that I think her boyfriend's an idiot. I don't really care. But the idea of her sleeping with that idiot seems weird to me, somehow inappropriate.

We're at her house-warming party. She and the idiot are standing together. It's just one room and the bed isn't big and it is obvious to me that anyone who shares this apartment and that bed with someone of the opposite sex must be having sex with them every day. Even though this is obvious it remains unimaginable and so I grab a handful of crisps from one of the porcelain bowls next to the idiot's record player and head, still chewing, for the toilet. When I get there, the idea that she shits in this toilet while the idiot goes about his idiot life on the other side of the door is even more unimaginable than the idea of her having sex with the idiot on a daily basis. I try to imagine the idiot taking a shit. No problem there.

We're at a club. I've broken up with my bipolar girlfriend, but we're still just friends. I look around nervously for one of my little sister's friends, or for someone else I could potentially go home with. We order drinks. She says, Would you like to dance, and I say, I'd rather stay here, and she says, All right then, stay here, I'll dance for you a little. She moves with grace and self-confidence, she has a smile on her face that tells me she is happy with herself and her body and with the effect the rhythm has on it. I look around for one of my little sister's friends, then I look back at her. She is still dancing. Others are dancing too. More and more people are dancing. When I can no longer see her amidst the other people dancing, I go home with one of my little sister's friends.

We don't kiss when she gets out

We're sitting in the car. It's our first date, but we don't know it yet because we're just friends. The night before this my bipolar ex cheated on her new boyfriend with me, and I left in the middle of the night because I suddenly realised that she wasn't the innocent little angel I had always made her out to be. We're sitting at a café in Schwabing and she passes the same verdict, and I know that I am finally over my bipolar ex. Then we pay and drive off, and I look through the windscreen at the women on the street and I ask her where we're going and she says, Just drive around a little. We just drive around a little. The car is well suited to just driving around. It's an old car with a long bonnet and it rides low. We pass the university beach bar but we don't get out, even though the people in the deckchairs look comfortable.

All around us is our home town, green, clean, and rich. Beautiful people, less beautiful people, insignificant people, the trees in front of the Maximilianeum, the noise of the cobblestones, the statues, a tunnel, bends in the road, the Angel of Peace.

We're listening to music. The sounds are attached to memories, which instantly disappear, replaced by a present that moments later becomes a memory. I sense a great calm on my right and I look over and she opens her eyes and says, Even as a kid I always fell asleep in the car. Then she shuts her eyes again. I don't know how long we've been driving or where else we could go, but at some point she says, Take me home, and I do.

We don't kiss when she gets out. She just smiles and says, That was fun, and with the words, I've got a present for you, she hands me something small, longish, rolled. It's a joint. And it's tight and warm because she's been holding it in her hand ever since we got in the car.

A weird direction

We're at the cinema. She's gorgeous. She's wearing a flowery skirt and her long black hair in a ponytail, and I like long black hair and flowery skirts. In the film, faces are smashed, brains blown out, legs chopped off, and there is a moment when I could kiss her, when she leans over to me and asks, Are you tired, and I jump because I'm so fixated on the guy with the butcher's knife who's looking to cut up the young blonde chick that I can't do anything except say No and then she leans back in her seat and I spend the rest of the film thinking if only I'd kissed her, and when Bruce Willis says, 'An old man dies, a young woman lives. Fair trade,' and then shoots himself in the head, I want to shoot myself in the head after saying something cool as well. After the film we go for a drink, she plays with her long black hair and is out of reach. Between us is the table, and on it a white wine spritzer and a wheat beer.

We go to an ice-cream parlour, our arms hanging down on either side of our bodies, our hands not touching. We've known each other for a long time, but not in the necessary way. We enter the ice-cream parlour. There's a free table. We order tall, complicated ice-cream sundaes with lots of whipped cream, even though I don't like cream, or tall, complicated sundaes, or ice cream, but she wants us to have ice cream, and so I want that too.

We're standing outside my door. We've gone out a few times in the past couple of weeks. Once I was half an hour late picking her up because I had run out of petrol. I ran to the petrol station, a kilometre, as fast as I could, I bought a jerry can and filled it, and ran back to the car with the jerry can full of petrol, I sweated and cursed and shouted: Why does this stuff always happen to me? We're standing outside my door because she doesn't want to come up, but she's got some DVDs I've asked to borrow, and I say, Why don't you come up, and she says she's got the feeling things are moving in a weird direction. I say, I don't think the direction is weird at all, and then she says that she does, and I at least manage to convince her not to leave right away, so we go to the playground across the street where there are ping pong tables set up under the tall beech trees. It's dark. We are sitting next to each other on a ping pong table and she says she doesn't want to get hurt and that I haven't got the best reputation and I'm annoyed that she's heard that I sometimes go home with random women and I say, But I've never enjoyed spending time with a woman like this before with no ulterior motive, and it's true, I know that for certain, because I've never spent time with a woman without having an ulterior motive. We talk a while longer and at some point she jumps down off the table and stands right up in front of me, and then we kiss, and she says, Don't let me go, and we hold each other tight.

I say yes

We're smoking marijuana. It's Christmas Eve. We smoke, and then we get undressed and dance around the living room to Crosby, Stills, Nash and Young. We stay naked and awake till the early morning. The apartment is well heated, and we eat and watch TV and laugh, and when I'm too tired she dances for me a little, and I lie on the sofa and watch her as she dances, and the smile on my face costs me no effort at all, it's just there, and just before my eyes fall shut, she comes closer, kneels down in front of the sofa and brings her face right up to mine, and I can see her eyes and hear her say, Are you happy?, and I say, Yes.

We are happy

We have sex. At first several times a day, then several times a week, then several times at the weekend, then once a week. We both enjoy it, we assure each other, we're just having less of it because there's a lot to do, we're stressed out, you've got to see your friends every once in a while.

We are beautiful. We are doing well. We like our bodies, our own and each other's, others think we're a good-looking couple. We are happy. We are what people call happy. We are what everyone we know calls happy. We have got what everyone wants, we do what everyone does. We have a total of €53,374.43 in the bank and could make a down payment on an apartment, a small one, and then pay off the mortgage, slowly, once we both got secure, permanent positions; they would need to be permanent for the credit rating, they would be secure because of our education, our friendly, reliable demeanour and our experience. We could take maternity leave, Germany is a civilised country that makes it possible for young parents to be young parents without severe financial repercussions, at least to begin with, not so much later on. Having a family is significantly more expensive than starting one, and after maternity leave your career is generally over, but you don't tell them that, not the children, because they wouldn't understand, and not the young parents, because they don't care about that at the moment. To them you say: That's wonderful.

We are standing on a stage

We're driving south on the Autobahn. We're on our way
to a village fair where she'll be singing. We're late and the
coolant begins to boil. We pull onto the hard shoulder
and I call the ADAC and then we wait, and I'm annoyed,
not only because I don't want to do this show and I'm
nervous because I'm supposed to accompany her on the
guitar, but also and especially because I know how much
it means to her and because I also know that that doesn't
cover it, that it also means a lot to me, which is why I'm
doing it. What's taking those yellow sons of bitches so
fucking long, I think, and she's singing prettyprettypretty-
please in a funny, childish way, and she squeezes my hand
tightly and just then those yellow sons of bitches finally
turn up.

We're standing on a stage. In front of us sit two hundred
people. She sings well, I don't fuck up. The applause is
genuine and long, she beams, and I think she's gorgeous
and it makes me proud to think that it's my primary
sexual organ that will be united with hers a little later.

We ride an elephant

We're on the plane, making a very bumpy approach to an island in Thailand, and she is holding my hand tightly because she knows I don't like flying, a formulation I use because I don't like saying I'm afraid of flying. I'm not really afraid of flying, it's rare that I'm truly nervous on an aeroplane, unless there's turbulence or Arabs in the cabin. I don't like the feeling of spatial confinement, of helplessness. She holds my hand and gives me a compassionate look, and the plane judders, and the island's peaks pierce the clouds. She squeezes my hand so tightly it hurts and I wonder if perhaps she's the one who's afraid and I give her a slightly irritated look which she interprets as a sign of my fear and squeezes my hand even more tightly, adding her other hand for support and I wonder what the guy sitting next to us must think. We land safely and I'm furious with her.

We're lying on the beach of an island in Thailand, she's getting a massage and I'm finishing Sloterdijk's *Critique of Cynical Reason*. I read the last three pages again, hoping this will allow me to say in one sentence what the book is about. She returns from her massage and asks, How was the book? and I say, Good, and she lies down next to me, not too close, she can sense my dissatisfaction, and I decide that it's a critique of idealism. I consider talking to her about it, about the unavoidable compulsion inherent in all idealistic systems to contradict themselves, either openly or in secret, but I hesitate, and I'm not sure whether I'm afraid she won't understand what I'm trying to say or whether I'm afraid I won't be able to say it. The next day, we ride an elephant.

She says she's not feeling well

We're at the Tegernsee. It's raining. She's not getting out of bed, and I'm looking out of the window. It's raining on the cosy wooden veranda, on which, on the evening of our arrival, exhausted from travelling, we shared a cigarette. It's raining on the dark green wooded cliffs beyond it. She says she's not feeling well, and I don't know if that means come here, or leave me alone. When the rain lets up we drive into town and have a coffee at a lakeside café. The lake is beautiful under the grey clouds. She's feeling a little better. Well enough to smoke. We talk a little and look out over the lake and then we go to the supermarket and I get a call from an old friend who wants to have a chat, but I cut the conversation short because I'm on holiday, with her, and I feel generous and loyal as I ring off and I look at her expectantly, but she just places a small jar of instant coffee in the shopping basket.

We're somewhere or other. Maybe at home, maybe out for breakfast, maybe at the wedding of a distant acquaintance who has invited us for nostalgia's sake. We're sitting or standing or leaning side by side against the wall of a ballroom or a school gymnasium or a provincial coaching inn and we're watching the people dance, and they either come up to me more often or to her because they either know her or me better. At some point we go outside for a cigarette.

We run into her ex-boyfriend. He's five years older than me, and I'm not yet old enough to perceive that as an advantage. He's tattooed and is a former paratrooper. The second thing he says to me is that he's bored at work, and the third is that in light of the unbelievable amount of money they pay him he can't bring himself to quit. They head off to the dance floor. I stay at the bar and wonder whether I should try to imagine what they used to get up to in bed together, but I'm too tired and so instead I stare at the barmaid's cleavage for a bit, but don't order anything.

We're lying in bed, it's the middle of the night, I've had beer and schnapps and wine to drink, we've had some friends over, she made a delicious pork roast and in the end we were all dancing on the sofa. She says she can't sleep because the words and the people are still buzzing around her head, but she's happy, she says, and she looks at me in the dark, as I lie there, crooked, numb and defenceless, and she leans over me and whispers in my ear, I love you. I pretend to be asleep.

We're watching football

I wake up. So does she. I throw the covers off. So does she. I get up. So does she. I take a shower, brush my teeth, get dressed. So does she. I drink a cup of coffee, I eat a pot of hazelnut yoghurt. So does she. I leave the house, walk down the street to the station, take the U-Bahn to Sendlinger Tor, change trains, get off at Implerstraße, walk up the steps and along Lindwurmstraße until I get to a large building with a sign that says Stemmerhof. So does she. I walk up the steps. So does she.

We're watching football. She's there too. We're watching football, and she's there too, because the We that is watching football is a different We than she and I. This We is mostly guys. We're watching football and she's there too, and the guys watching with me are various heights and ages, and close to me in varying degrees. They've known me longer, know me differently and better than she will ever know me, but this knowledge and this being known has no consequences except for the one, single consequence that we have always drawn from it, which is that we are here, all of us together, just as we always were. But still at some point we will all be alone, I think, and then no one will be here except for her.

We are standing in an artist's studio, it's a big studio, there are lots of us, fifty, sixty people, the canvases, paint cans and balls of paper have been cleared away, in their place there are old armchairs and cushions and cases of beer and us. We are wearing the colours of the team that we want to see win, they are our national colours, and we wear them with more seriousness than the situation calls for: it's a game. We are shouting. It's not a game.

We are shouting and the other team walks onto the pitch, which is to say the wall of the studio, and they are wearing different colours and have different faces and shoulders and backs and calves from our players. We don't know them as well as we know our players. We know our players' bodies, their faces, their names, their voices, their gait. We know our players better than she will ever know me. They don't know that, and she doesn't know it either. She will never know, that's what makes her her, after all.

We hear the whistle, and we see the movements of the players we know. We know their movements, even when they haven't got the ball, and when they have got the ball, we shout. They run; we shout. They stumble; we shout.

They fall; we shout. And then they get back up again. We shout, the ball flies through the air, we shout, and they run and move the ball upfield, closer and closer to the other team's goal, and then suddenly the ball is in the back of the very net we always wanted it to be in, will always want it to be in, and we shout and jump and they jump and shout and embrace, pat each other on the back and on the shoulder and on the chest and rub their heads and slap themselves for joy, fury, pride and hatred of their common enemy, and I give her a kiss on the cheek.

We shout, *Deutschland*. So does she. We clink our thick brown beer bottles together as hard as we can without breaking them. So does she. We thrust our fists in the air. So does she. We chant, Na na na na hey hey hey goodbye. So does she. We sing Olé olé-olé-olé. So does she. We watch our players run, we watch as they tackle the other players, and we watch how one of the other players writhes in pain, and then we shout, Drama queen. She takes a sip from her bottle. She doesn't really like beer. And then we watch as our opponents lose the ball again and we roar, our roar rising up like a wall against the wall with the flickering images, and then our players run with the ball deep into the other team's territory and then the ball is at the back of the net again, and we're shouting, slapping, jumping and crying, as is she.
And then we hear the whistle. Sweden have lost two–nil.

Everyone is running onto the field, and we're jumping and falling and piling on top of each other and then we rush out of the studio and head for the U-Bahn station, decked out in all our colours, as is she, with flags a-waving, and we stand and drink and laugh and the beer bottles clink and then the train arrives and in it are two people wearing Swedish colours and we see them and we chant at the top of our lungs: Na na na na hey hey hey goodbye. She's singing, as well. We take the train to Schwabing, and then we pour out onto Leopoldstraße, dissolve into it, and suddenly all the others are gone and at the same time they're everywhere, the others are everyone, the colours and flags and bottles and shouts. I take off my jersey and tuck it into the front of my trousers and I stuff the end of my black-red-and-gold flag into my back pocket so it hangs behind me, and then I climb onto a traffic light and I'm sitting high above the crossing and holding on to the sun-warmed metal with both hands. From my arse hangs the flag of the Federal Republic of Germany and underneath me is a sea of exactly the same colours as the ones hanging out of my trousers and then I shout *Deutschland*. I don't shout it quite as loudly as I could have because I know she's down there somewhere and she's looking up at me and thinking, now he's sitting on a traffic light and shouting *Deutschland*.

She knows me and she likes me anyway

We want to get away from the daily grind. We drive out of the city, into the countryside, to be by a lake. We can't find a parking space. There are cars parked everywhere on these luscious fields. Half-naked people in flip-flops shuffle by, carrying blankets and cool boxes. It's intolerably hot, and when we finally park at the edge of the field, so close to another car that I have to get out on the passenger side, the electric window stops working. I take note of this, leave the window down and think no more of it, but she is worried about the car, my car, for my sake. All I want to do is get the towels and the flip-flops and the water bottle and my swimming trunks out of the boot as quickly as possible and then get away from the car and the field, out of the sun, to the water and then get away from the lake and go home again, or somewhere, anywhere where there are no people and the air isn't as oppressive. Everyone says they love this heat. At last a proper summer, they say. She is wearing nothing but a thin summer dress, but I don't believe anyone who claims they like it when the air around you is hotter than your blood. Oh dear, she says and strokes my arm because she's sorry I've had to leave the car window down, and because she knows how little I enjoy the sun and the heat and the lake. Her sympathy is both nice and unnerving because it tells me that she knows me and she likes me anyway.

Early in the morning, we are standing on the crowded U-Bahn train. We kiss and she gets off at the station before mine. As the doors close I keep looking in her direction because I assume she will turn around and I don't want her to turn around and see that I'm no longer looking. And so I look. She doesn't turn around.

A bedtime story

We're in a taxi on our way to a karaoke bar because she likes to sing and I like to drink. The taxi driver throws a fit when a news bulletin about the introduction of tuition fees comes on the radio, and says that after this trip she's taking a break. She drops us off at the place in Schwabing, turns the taximeter off and doesn't turn her light back on. We enter the bar, order drinks. On the stage a guy who looks like a lawyer is singing Elvis. We drink gin and tonic. Before long, she is up on stage and her voice is so clear and bright and lovely that I consider crying at the impossibility of holding onto this moment and calling it up the next time I get a letter from the taxman, the next time I wake up with bad breath and a hangover, the next time we have breakfast in silence, or the next time we go and hang out with her friends, who are nice and every-thing, but, well, you know. I think I really could start to cry if I spent long enough thinking about her bright, clear voice, her eyes gazing intently and hopefully in my direction, her slender, healthy body which she knows is beautiful and which really is beautiful for that very reason.

Right now thirty other pairs of male eyes are seeking her gaze but they are only staring into space, because at this moment she is standing there, singing, and breathing, for me alone. But it's all in vain. Not because my heart is too hard, but because it is too soft, much too soft, a sponge, a cloud in a grey sky, and I take a sip of gin and tonic and she returns triumphantly to our table and I kiss her on the cheek and put my arm around her and pull her in close, my fingers gripping her shoulder tightly, but the only thing I'm trying to hold onto is myself.

Later that evening, we're lying on the sofa watching TV, and taking turns nodding off. When at last we're both awake at the same time, we decide to go to bed.

We hold each other tightly. We let go. One of us always holds on a little more tightly than the other, one of us always lets go a little sooner than the other. We orbit each other in unpredictable circles and although I love you is nothing but a bedtime story now, it's a bedtime story that still works.

We decide we should do nice things more often

We go for a walk. It is raining and it becomes tiresome moving through the falling water. We are walking uphill. We are in a village in Upper Bavaria and it is a strange time of year to be in a mountain village in Upper Bavaria, because there is no snow yet, or none left, and it's no longer warm and pleasant, or not yet warm and pleasant. Occasionally, we make out a spectacular cloud formation in a slightly darker grey than the standard, matte grey of the background. The sky looks like it still has a lot left to drop on us. We're wearing plastic jackets and hiking boots and we're walking uphill, but we're not really in the mountains yet, and when the water starts falling harder and harder, penetrating the gaps in our plastic jackets through to our skin and into our hiking boots, we turn. We turn, after having walked uphill across empty meadows where the water pools as if the rain were coming up from below. We walk along mostly electrified, well-kept fences. The meadows are endless and slope gently upwards. In the distance, sparsely vegetated cliffs rise up into the clouds, grey, porous, massive.

We take the turn for the gorge, Leutasch or Partnach, and the path grows steeper. A walk in the rain turns into a hike in the mountains. We walk along the cliff face and it stops raining, then it starts again. The cliffs come closer to the path, or the path to the cliffs. We walk on, and after half an hour the opposite cliff face also comes closer. I wonder what the difference is between a ravine and a gorge, and then both cliff faces come closer and grow sheerer, almost meeting each other before falling sharply away, and then there is a little brown cabin, and we pay some money to a fat man and we're inside. Everything sounds different, everything seems different, there are steel cables attached to steel supports embedded in concrete. We hold on to a cable, inching along the abyss where, down below, a trickling stream has become a raging river, foaming and loud. It is impossible to drown here, because if you were to fall, you would have other things to worry about besides getting water in your lungs. Water drips from the overhanging rocks, which I have to duck to pass under, but she does not, she's shorter than me. On the other side trees grow at physically impossible angles directly out of the rock face. The sky is no longer visible, there is only rock, green, and water. We walk on, it grows darker, narrower, wetter, louder. I have long since stopped being able to tell where the sound of the rain ends and that of the stream begins, or whether the noise here is simply the sound of narrowness and stone, and then suddenly she stops, right in front of me, and she turns around and opens her mouth, and I shout, What? and she opens her mouth again, but I hear only water and narrowness and stone, and then I bend over and hold my ear directly in front of her mouth and she shouts, I'm pregnant.

We're at her mother's, and we decide to terminate the pregnancy. Her mother decides this. Her father stays out of it, and I'm too proud and numbed to do anything at all, too proud and numbed by the unconditional commitment I made to her a few days earlier, by my solemn oath to stand by her, no matter what she decides. We'll get through this, together, we'll raise a child together or pull a child out of your body and throw it away, whatever you want, darling.

I rent a car with winter tyres, because it snowed the night before and my car only has summer tyres. We drive to the abortion clinic. The doctor is nice and professional and pragmatic. She takes a pill and drinks a sip of water, and that's that. Then we drive to her parents' place and we play Nintendo for three days, Super Mario Kart, and every now and then she presses pause and gets up to go and flush a bit of dead organic material from her womb down the toilet.

We understand each other. We feel rage. We experience rejection. Later, we talk about rejection until it dissolves into a to and fro of new behavioural patterns and old habits, and we say, But you know that I love you, and then we understand each other again. We relinquish demands that have to do with pride or uncertainty, and sometimes we drive away the uncertainty with sex, but mostly we're too tired.

We're watching 24. It's three o'clock in the morning, she's asleep and we have to get up at seven-thirty, but I put the next DVD in the tray all the same and roll another joint. She sleeps, I smoke, and suddenly the theme music seems much too loud and too pathos-ridden, too manipulative, too action-packed. Jack Bauer's torture methods are a bit too repetitive, and the ultimate threat to Western civili-sation is a little too ultimate, or maybe I'm just too tired and stoned, so I turn off the TV and the light and kiss her on the cheek and say, Shall we go to bed? She goes, Mmm-hmm, I'll be right there, and, What time is it? and I say, It's late. I know she will fall asleep the second I leave the room, and that she will sleep on the sofa and at some point she will come to bed, that she'll be tired and disappointed I didn't wake her, and at five o'clock she comes in and says, Why didn't you wake me?

We say goodbye. We're standing by an escalator. We

give each other a quick kiss on the lips, or perhaps not even on the lips, on the cheek, the forehead, or not at all. We hug less tightly, for less long, and let go, one sooner than the other. We look at each other just before we turn away, then we lower our gaze before it breaks, so that we can view this separation as an autonomous decision by two mature people and not as the logical consequence of bodies in motion, atoms in gas. Beforehand, we go over it all again. The non-existent reasons for modes of behaviour that don't matter to me but matter to her a great deal, or vice versa. Or the modes of behaviour whose significance she or I couldn't or wouldn't see, out of incapacity or fear or hope, in an effort to cling to and believe in a world we invented together, long ago. We are standing by the escalator, she doesn't ask me anything, I don't say anything, and so we just stand there, and then at some point we take the escalator down, we walk across the mezzanine, past people who don't know anything, and we take the next escalator down and then we stand together in silence on the platform, and in her eyes there is trust and a clarity that reassures me, and something else, I'm not sure what it is, and we wait and look at each other, and my train arrives first.

I'M SORRY

I am deeply moved and very tired

We're in New York. I'm standing in the arrivals hall at the airport and the first thing I see is her beautiful legs. She's wearing tight grey jeans, light brown leather boots and gold earrings. Her long, black hair is pulled severely back and she is pulling her heavy suitcase along behind her. Something lights up in her eyes when she sees me. But she controls herself and glances away again. She walks on, past people of different skin-colours and shapes, her gait light and easy as always, another thirty metres, ten, five. She ducks under the barrier separating the people arriving from the people there to pick them up because apparently she's too impatient to walk all the way to the end, she's been travelling for long enough, and now at last she is standing before me. She laughs, we kiss, and I want to fuck her. I don't tell her so right away, of course, instead we kiss some more and I ask, How was your flight?, and suddenly my field of vision narrows. I can see her dark eyes. I can see one of her bra straps. The collar of her T-shirt is broad and has slipped a little. I see a strand of hair above her ear that has come loose from her plait.

I see a vending machine.

Are you thirsty?

Yes.

Wait here, I'll get you something.

I get water and a bottle of pink liquid, a new American drink that we've talked about at home occasionally. She always said she would be curious to see how it tasted and that when she was here, she'd like to try one. She gives me a grateful look as I hand her the bottle, and she can barely drink it because it's so cold, and I really like the way she says, Ooh, cold.

We're sitting side by side on the train. She smells faintly of sweat, but I don't care. I know that smell, it's just been a while. When I point out the Manhattan skyline beyond the empty harbour and industrial ruins of Newark she is very excited, and I think that from now on I can and will and must be there for her, and suddenly I am deeply moved by her belief that everything can work out for the best as long as you try, it's hard work but it pays off. I am deeply moved and very tired. When we get back to my place we have sex and after the first orgasm I am happy because she is so excited when she looks out of the window and so happy to be here with me.

It's all right

We're at my apartment. She's sitting on the sofa and is happy that I've come home from work, and I feel empty and tired and angry because her joy makes me aware of my emptiness and tiredness and anger. And because I don't want to tell her that I hate myself, I say, Philosophy sucks. She asks if I'm having trouble with my lecture and hands me a cigarette and then she walks ahead of me out of the apartment, along the corridor and into the stairwell where she sits down on the stairs and gives me a light. The walk to the stairwell calms me down a bit. I say, It's all right. I take a drag on my cigarette. She waits to see if there's more, and when I don't say anything she slowly nods and takes a drag herself. Smoke pours out of her nostrils. Then she smiles proudly, looks me straight in the eye and says, Today I walked across the Williamsburg Bridge. I'm happy she's here and that she did that and I'm sad because I wasn't there with her, but then it occurs to me that if I had been, I would just have spent the whole time thinking about my lecture or about other women, and so I say nothing and take another drag on my cigarette, and with my other hand I gently stroke her cheek, even though she's quite calm, and she lets me, because she knows it calms me down.

I wonder if I should quit smoking

We're walking past warehouses. Those gigantic Williamsburg warehouses with the rusty rolling gates, which are sometimes open, in which case someone will be there loading worn-out old mattresses with mildew stains onto a pick-up truck, and I envy those men who find satisfaction in taking used mattresses from warehouses with rusty gates and loading them onto pick-up trucks and driving them somewhere else and unloading them again. Men who do their job without hesitating, happy simply because it would never even occur to them to wonder if their job makes them happy or not. I wonder if I should tell her that I have no talent for being happy. I wonder if I should tell her that I'm only happy when I'm not wondering if I'm happy, and that I'm basically always wondering if I'm happy, except when I'm eating, drinking, shitting or coming. And sometimes, when I take a breath and the air is cool and clean. I wonder if I should quit smoking. I wonder if I should tell her that I want to do something important. Something that means something. Something that will make the world a better place. Something that would advance the human race. I wonder if I should tell her that there are moments when I believe that the philosophical problem of consciousness might be solvable and that I might be the one to solve it. Then I wonder if I should tell her that I don't think we should have children because I find myself more intolerable the more people I have around me, but she strokes my forearm and says, You've caught the sun. Then I wonder if I should tell her that I've got a mental defect, that I just can't control my thoughts, that I've got some kind of analytic Tourette's syndrome. And I say to her, So have you. I wonder if I should tell her something about the lecture I'm supposed to be giving soon, but I let it go.

We walk across the Manhattan Bridge. We see young families in the park by the East River. Mothers playing ball with their children. They're too far away for me to be able to tell if they're pretty, but I can tell that some of them have got big breasts.
Look at the children.
Yeah.

A rainbow

After the park comes the water, after the water, the opposite shore, behind it the skyline in silhouette, so unreal and overwhelming and clichéd that I try to ignore it. Leaving the bridge, we enter Chinatown. We walk down a long set of stairs, past a confusion of roofs covered in illegible graffiti. Somewhere down there we will soon be having Peking duck. She knows where, she's found the best places for Peking duck in her guidebook.

We enter the restaurant, find a table, and when I notice her childlike excitement, I get a warm feeling in my stomach, and just at the moment when I sense this feeling clearly enough to be able to articulate it, I look down at it, invalidate it by virtue of the fact that I am also thinking about other things, articulating other things, that other things are piling up inside me, like for instance, what the hell, don't be so loud, wankers, slant-eyes, tits, again, and beer. And cigarettes, of course, and why does everyone love this city so much, all it is is big and full of people, and while all of these things are flying around inside me, she looks around inquisitively and excitedly and my stomach no longer feels quite so warm. She gives me a grateful smile and we eat and it's good and we pay the bill and leave. Outside, she takes my hand and holds it tightly, swinging it back and forth in time with her confident steps. She strides through this city and through her life, and I walk alongside her and can't even tell if my feet are touching the ground. She looks around inquisitively and drinks in the things all around us, things she knew would be here waiting for her, things she was already thinking about on the plane, wondering what it looked like here, what it smelled and sounded like, the fish at the Chinese street-vendors' stalls, the sound of the reversing lorries, the colourful massage-parlour windows and the countless T-shirts for sale by the side of the road, arranged according to colour. A rainbow named I ♥ New York. I think: gay.

I think, to think that she was already thinking about these things on the aeroplane as she read about them in the book she bought after booking the flight. She was already thinking about the bridges, the skyscrapers, the snow-white magnolia bushes, the Statue of Liberty, the East Village. She was already thinking about medium-rare roast beef at Katz's. On my flight I was thinking about explosions, and whether if you were at the epicentre of one you would primarily experience heat or sound before you stopped experiencing anything at all, and whether you would be able to experience the moment in which you realise that in a moment's time you will no longer experience anything at all.

On my flight I was wondering whether I would be able to stay faithful to her, and whether I even wanted to, and why, if I didn't want to, I should even try, and whether I should call her the minute I landed and tell her that I wasn't going to be able to make it work. But I didn't pursue these thoughts, or at some point they just vanished of their own accord, probably because as I dozed in the dry air of the cabin I started thinking about her eyes, and how they brush over me, in mundane situations in everyday places, they brush over me briefly, just ever so briefly, but they hold me completely, because they are wide open, they are big, and they are full of wonder, and they dart from one thing to the next and draw everything in. They see the world, and they see that it is beautiful, even though there is a lot out there that's a bit strange or difficult to understand. They see that on the whole everything is all right. It's OK, you're OK world, say her big, brave eyes when they brush over it, and then they brush over me as well, and suddenly there I am, feet firmly on the ground, a part of this solar system, and I know: somewhere in her field of vision is where I belong. And then I start thinking about other women's sexual organs.

Our friends

It's her birthday. We're at the Sky Bar at the Standard Hotel. It's 5:42 p.m., and we can stay at this table till six. After that it's only for people who've made reservations, using a telephone number no one knows and which no one will give you. The décor is conspicuously discreet, almost offensively tasteful. There is a silent gas flame in a lily-white fireplace, and lots of pastel colours everywhere: the thick, fluffy carpet, the bar, the tables, the tablecloths, the chairs we're sitting on, the cocktail dresses the waitresses are wearing. The waitresses are thin and about as tall as I am – and I'm tall – plus, without exception, they're all stunningly beautiful. The walls are also pastel-coloured, and the shoes and trousers and blazers the other guests are wearing, and my hand on hers, and her eyes, and the sky outside the enormous glass façade.

I say, Happy birthday. She smiles. She orders another.
What time do we need to be on 5th Avenue?
In about an hour.
We've got time.

Yes.

I order another too. We drink quickly and at 6:02 p.m., we leave the Standard Hotel via the revolving door. We walk across the High Line, we see how green and renovated it all is, how tastefully and innovatively designed, and we see the Hudson and beyond it New Jersey, and then we get on the subway. We get off at Fifth Avenue and take the lift to another bar, a bar where you can look up the phone number, where you can call and book a table, a table you can stay at after six o'clock. This bar is darker and bigger. There are no pastel colours here, just black and red. As if deposited by crane, massive seating islands are scattered around the space, dark leather and square, arranged around square tables, and from the ceiling hang cubes of flatscreen TVs showing various soundless sporting events.

The two of us are occupying one of these gigantic leather sofa squares, waiting, relieved that our friends will be arriving soon. People are already giving us dirty looks for taking up so much space, just the two of us. There will be more of us, hopefully soon. We're waiting for our friends from Munich, they used to be her friends, now they are our friends, friends with whom she once shared a great many experiences and with whom we now never experience anything, friends who say, When you're visiting him in New York, we'll come and visit you, who knows when you'll ever be in New York again, New York isn't somewhere you go every day and besides, it's your birthday. Can we stay with you?

We wait. Out of the corner of my eye I can see one of the TV screens in a nearby cube. I see people moving across an American football field. Their movements are somehow different from the norm, something is different, so I turn and look more closely and I see that they are women, and they're only wearing underwear, and I quickly turn and look away.

Look: the Lingerie League, she says, and so I look again, and together we stare at the screen and we see two teams of lingerie models slamming their breasts and arses and thighs together, their flowing hair underneath their helmets, their full, soft lips. I try to imagine them shouting.

Then our friends arrive. There are fewer of them than we expected. In Iceland some mountain or other has exploded, the sky was too dirty to fly, but a couple have made it, and now they are here, and they're standing in the entrance looking determined and somewhat helpless, and then they spot us and storm up and embrace her and me too.

How are you, says one.

Yeah, how are you, says the other.

Good, I say, thanks.

Thanks, good, says she.

And how are you? I say.

Good. Thanks.

Fancy meeting you here in New York, says one, and they pat me on the shoulder, and outside the window the Empire State Building glows.

And happy birthday, says the other, she says Thank you and they get up and kiss each other on the cheek, and then we sit back down, and I put my hand on her thigh.

Hey, the Lingerie League, says one, Haha, says the other, and if none of them were there I would spend the next hour staring with rapt attention at the lingerie models slamming their breasts, arses and thighs into each other, but instead I just laugh in a very adult and somewhat condescending way, and I say, Only in America.

We drink beer. We drink cocktails. We watch the Lingerie League with one eye. We eat finger food. We drink cocktails. At some point we go out into the street, we smoke cigarettes and embrace out of drunkenness and enthusiasm, we hold each other tight, all four of us, our two friends and she and I, and we see the lights and feel the alcohol and at some point a taxi pulls up next to us and takes us to Brooklyn. Our friends sleep on the sofa bed, they start snoring almost immediately, soon she is snoring too, because she snores. Everybody snores, except me. I lie awake and wonder why I'm not happy to have so many friendly people in my life.

The next day, we go to the top of the Rockefeller Center. We have bratwurst and Augustiner beer at a German place in the East Village. We go to MoMA. We go to a party at a friend of my landlord's place in DUMBO. There are vegan cocktails. We take the Staten Island Ferry to Staten Island. We fly in a helicopter over Manhattan. We go to a photo exhibition at a tiny gallery and we feel superior to the other visitors because the photographer is a friend of a friend's ex-girlfriend. We go to Central Park and lie down on the grass. It's the first hot day of the year. We go to a Mets game. We eat hotdogs. We drink beer. After four hours, someone hits a home run. After a week of this we take our friends to the airport.

I refuse to believe it is evil

We're alone again. We sit on a park bench by the East River. We see an abandoned sugar refinery. We see several cargo ships go by. We walk along Bedford Avenue. We visit a small, alternative bookshop. We go home. We smoke in the stairwell. We look out of the window. We look at the Williamsburg Bridge. We listen to the Italian girl in the apartment upstairs on the phone with her father. We have sex. We fall asleep next to each other.

It is physically impossible for me to ignore the appearance of a female body within my field of vision. I cannot avoid the photons that strike my eyeballs, carrying in them messages formed of skin and curve and muscle. I cannot prevent an image from forming on my retina. I cannot stop my brain from deciphering it. I cannot halt the chain of associations, memories and fantasies from when I was twelve to this very moment, and the next, and the next. I cannot undo the fact that I was conceived, born, and raised. There's nothing I can do to change the fact that I have a Y-chromosome.

I refuse to believe it is evil to seek release from one's urges not in religion, or by claiming illness, but in front of the computer. I refuse to apologise for being a man, in the biological sense. I will not go on denying that I want to fuck every – and I mean every – woman under the age of fifty who weighs under eighty kilos and has a halfway attractive face. I object to the implication that my love for her is less real just because of this boring, unalterable fact.

The fact that I want to fuck other women does not mean that we have to break up. The fact that I want to fuck other women does not mean that the society we live in is hypersexualised, manipulated by advertising, or dumbed-down and debauched. The fact that I want to fuck other women does not mean that she is ugly, or that I am sick, or that we couldn't live happily ever after and die arm in arm. The fact that I want to fuck other women doesn't even mean that I really want to fuck other women, but more likely just that something in me wants to fuck something else, and since I don't know anything else, I fill in the blanks with *I* and *women*. The fact that I want to fuck other women means absolutely nothing. It's completely normal. Hormones. Carbon. Water.

What's the matter?

I wake up with a start. It's dark. My T-shirt is stuck to my chest. Above me, below the black ceiling, I see an oval of even blacker, much, much closer blackness. She strokes my forehead.

Nothing.
Is everything OK?
Yes.

I don't not care about anything

We go out for a bit. I pat my pockets looking for cigarettes, and meanwhile she holds her hand out impatiently for me to hold when I've finally found my cigarettes. I don't find any. I take her hand anyway. In a doorway lies a dog.
Look, a dog, she says.
Mm-hmm.
We stop for a moment in front of the Jewish supermarket on the corner while we make up our minds whether to turn right or left. On the right is the harbour, on the left are the Puerto Rican housing projects, and I say, Do you want to go down to the harbour or over to the Puerto Rican housing projects, and she lays her head on my shoulder and says, Whichever, I don't care.
She turns and stands in front of me. I look in the direction of the harbour. She squeezes my hand even harder than she normally does. I look in the direction of the Puerto Rican housing projects. She puts her free arm around my hips. I look back the way we've just come, she pulls me closer and kisses my shoulder through my jacket. I kiss the top of her head and look at the Jewish supermarket,

and then I say, Do we need anything?

No.

She lets go of my hand and puts her other arm around my hips, she holds me tightly, and I hug her back. I'm taller, and I am careful to hold her tightly enough to communicate love, but not so tightly that she feels trapped. In response, she squeezes me even more tightly. I feel trapped.

Let's go down to the harbour, I say.

Yes, she says.

We walk in the direction of the harbour. After walking for two hours with a busy street on our right and to our left a six-foot-tall chain-link fence topped with barbed wire, and, beyond that, thickets and warehouses and dilapidated captain's houses, we decide that the Brooklyn Navy Yard is much too big to walk around and much too fenced off to access, so we turn around. Above the inaccessible area, spectacular clouds.

Look! The clouds.

Mm-hmm.

That night she wakes up and says, Do you really think you're alone in the world?

What?

Do you really think you're alone in the world?

Outside my window, the lights of eight million people.

No.

But what purpose do you see in what you do, besides the desire to prove to yourself that you can do it? You don't care about philosophy. You don't care about me, either. You basically don't care about anything.

I don't not care about anything.

She breathes.

Do you want me to go?

No.

Why should I believe you?

I don't know. I can't force you to believe me. I can't convince you. I can only hope you do. I hope that you believe me. Because the alternative would be awful. Because if you don't believe me when I say that I want you to stay, that must mean you assume I'm lying. And if I am lying, you would have to assume that I've lied to you many times before, at similar moments, and then what would our love be worth?

She says nothing. I can hear her breathing in the darkness. I can see the outline of her head against the city lights. It is moving. She is nodding.

You're right. If you are lying now, you have probably lied many times before. In which case we are only still together because you're afraid of hurting me.

I feel hot.

And that can't be.

Exactly.

She lies back down. Slowly, I edge over to her, I put my arm by her head, she rests it on it, I come still closer, I insert my arm under her head, and she rests it on my chest.

We breathe.

Look. You'll be leaving in four days anyway, I say, and immediately I feel hot again. I'm stunned, I can't believe I've just said that, after everything I've just been saying, after everything I've said in the past two years, over and over again. I know she is stunned too, but I also know that she won't say anything, not today, not tomorrow, never again, and my only consolation in this moment is that I know for certain that I am just as surprised as she is.

I feel her nodding. She nods slowly and breathes carefully, as if something might break, and she nods and breathes and nods and breathes, and suddenly her head on my chest feels very small and wet.

Unlikely combinations

We go and see a musical. A guy in a mask is singing about love or its loss or the desire for it, for love or for its loss. Sometimes she hums along. When she notices that I've noticed, she jumps. Broadway is smaller than I had imagined, smaller than the name suggests. The theatre, on the other hand, seems much bigger on the inside than it looks from the outside. The rows of seats are higher and more numerous, the felt-upholstered wooden seats feel strangely plastic and hollow, they have ornaments that don't seem to belong to any period, and I can't decide if they're tacky or if I'm just channelling European cultural pseudo-superiority. As I take my seat, I think that without America we would all be either Nazis, or farmers, or dead. Before I can think about what it is that we have become *with* America, she says how lovely it is to be here with me and she takes my hand and squeezes it tightly. I squeeze back.

We go to a rooftop bar in SoHo. We're wearing bright red, hooded, fleece jackets. It looks funny. All the guests are wearing them, it's cold and there are over a hundred hanging by the stairs. The Empire State Building shines less brightly, high up and far away. Maybe that's why people go to rooftop bars, or into the mountains, or even out onto the pavement. So that you feel bigger and the world feels smaller.

We drink cocktails and smoke. It's permitted here, we're outside. Fairy lights that remind me of Christmas hang from the palm-like potted plants. Perhaps America is, above all, the land of unlikely combinations. Like her and me. And adenine, cytosine, guanine, thymine.

Biological explanations

We're at my apartment. I'm reading an email from a friend of a friend of a friend. His name is John and I have no idea what he does, only that he lives in New York and his birthday is coming up, or that it's just been, or it's right now. The email says:

Birthday Bash East 9th Street, Avenue A.

Want to go to a party?
Sure. You?
I plonk myself down on the sofa. I wonder why I would want to go to a party where I don't know anyone and then I think that there will almost certainly be women there. I don't think about the colour of their hair, or their figures, or their clothes, but just that one word, women, and then I think that this is stupid because I won't be going alone and even if I were going alone, well, whatever. And then I think how simple biological explanations are, the idea that everything we do, we do in order to reproduce, and then we don't end up reproducing after all, or don't want to, or do we? What do we

want, really? If we just wanted to reproduce, we could do that at home.

Yeah, I'm game.

Great.

I wonder if perhaps having a baby would solve all our problems. When you've got a kid you spend less money on alcohol and cigarettes. You have fewer opportunities to masturbate. With a kid, you can't leave the *Goldberg Variations* playing on Sundays for long enough for you to get sick of them. With a kid, you don't notice how much crap people do and write because you would have to put the newspaper down before you'd had a chance to finish reading that article, because someone else would be there, someone new, and this someone would want something and get it, and all the financial crises and the debates about integration and the wars on the planet would appear just as small and insignificant as the time of day, that arbitrary epiphenomenon of the present, that unit of measurement for reality. For a reality that is boring enough to be measurable. I close my eyes.

Are you tired?

A little.

But we're going to that party, right?

Yeah.

While she decides what to wear, I think that maybe the problem with that screaming kid at the restaurant was that it wasn't my own. My kid doesn't exist, even though in theory there could already be lots of my kids out there.

Which do you prefer?

That one.

While she puts on the dress that I prefer, I think about masturbation. Not about doing it myself, but about masturbation in the abstract. About the billions of potential Nobel laureates, warlords and child molesters who die every day, all over the world, in a tissue, a sock, an old T-shirt, or in the hair on someone's belly.

Do these shoes go with my dress?

Yes.

She starts putting on make-up, and I think about sexual intercourse. About contraception. About armies of haploid sets of chromosomes skulking around cervixes for a while before seeping out again, having been led to believe that one of them would win the race, when in fact the race has been cancelled by a pill. Then I think about walls of latex and the duds that smash into them and later dry up, damp squibs that don't even really make it out of the body whose uniqueness they are supposed to transmit into the outside world, with its talents and hereditary diseases and its potentially stupid face.

Shall we go?

The world without us

We're at a club, the music is going bam bam and we're fighting our way to the bar, she's pushing aside hips and I'm pushing aside shoulders and then we're leaning on the bar with the crowd at our backs and at some point I shout, Gin and tonic and hold two fingers in the air, and shortly afterwards a man puts two glasses in front of us, we pay, and suddenly it's mission accomplished. One at a time, we're washed away from the bar which we'd reached as a unit, fighting through strange smells, past strange bodies and clothes, and eyes that wanted to look at us but couldn't, as if they were sliding off the indissoluble block that was us when we both wanted the same thing, a gin and tonic. Now that we have it, they're no longer interested in us. We're no longer interested in us either.

I find it hard to take. I want to say something, so I say I'm sorry.

What?

The music goes bam bam.

I'm sorry.

I heard you. Sorry about what?

Everything.

A-ha.

I drink, and look away again, and I'm a little disappointed because I had the feeling I was making a fairly funda-mental confession, and I expected some kind of reaction, I don't know what, but in any case more than an a-ha. The music goes bam bam, and she tenses up, perhaps she's seen something in my face, in any case she gently squeezes my arm and says it's OK and tries to smile. So do I. Then we each turn our heads towards the dance floor and I can see in her eyes that as soon as our gazes separate we will see different things, forever, and then our gazes do separate, and we look straight ahead and I see shards, shoes, tits and arses and I have no idea what she's seeing. It's not us who are seeing what's in front of us anymore. I see something, she sees something. And I think, so that was that, then.

We're in the taxi and I'm thinking so that was that, then, and I say the world is fucked up. She says, That's too easy. I say, The world is too complex. She says, That's too imprecise. I say, That's exactly what I mean, and she says, What exactly do you mean by that?

I mean the future. The past. The missed opportunities. The possibilities. It's all too much.

Yes.

Every car coming from the other direction could smash into us.

So?

So then we'd be dead. Instantaneously. Just like that.

So? Then we'd be dead.

No. You don't understand what that means. Being alive. It means being somewhere. And at some point you won't be anywhere anymore. That's it. The world will still be there without us.

I'm saying I know all that, and I think that we can't know, that we will never know, what will be there after we die.

She says nothing more that evening.

We decide to do something nice again

It snows again overnight. We're standing at Penn Station. We see soldiers in computer-generated camouflage and Kevlar helmets holding their machine guns in front of their chests to warn off carriers of suspicious suitcases. We get on a train that takes us out of the city through long tunnels into the middle of a radiant white. It's a different white than in the city, it begins after Jamaica Bay. As sky, the white makes your eyes shrink, as snow, your pores. From the branches of the broom shrubs it looms over our heads. We're going to the seaside. It really is too cold to go to the seaside.

We walk along the street with the wind in our faces. Occasionally a car passes, the drivers staring at us like we're runaway livestock. We walk on. All around us, evenly spread out, are houses that are only inhabited in the summer. What are we doing here again? It's beautiful. We each know that the wind is hurting the other's eyes and ears at least as much as our own, and that with the cold each of us is growing more uncertain. How much further? Is this the right way? We walk on, along broad, gently serpentine drives for summerhouse owners in their roadsters and SUVs, over hills, past bushes and houses. We are walking along a dirty yellow line at the side of the road. It's the only colour that doesn't hurt here, even the tarmac glistens cold and hard, and the stones embedded in the surface look like they've been individually polished, even though they're probably quite coarse. We don't bend down and touch them. We want to get to the beach. We haven't said a word to each other since the hotel where we wanted to get a hot drink. It was closed. On the train we talked about this and that. Mutual friends, our parents, our siblings, other people we like more, or less, or differently than each other. On the train we were happy. And right now we are happy, actually. We have had enough to eat, our clothes are sufficiently warm and our shoes are sufficiently sturdy. We are going to a seaside resort in what feels like minus ten degrees. We squint. The white is becoming unbearable. I look around, try to smile, apologise for the cold and for the fact that one of us had the idea to come out here.

Lovely, these bushes, don't you think?

Yes. Lovely.

We reach the town square, which would be bigger than the town if there weren't so much space between the houses. It's round, so drivers can turn easily when they see there's nothing here. We walk on.

As we near the top of a small hill, we see a gap open up with a long row of houses on either side. We follow a path until we're less than twenty yards away from the water's edge, and only then does the sound of the ocean drown out the sound of the wind. The light is denser than we are, a solid block containing everything, penetrating everything. We stand side by side, before us the Atlantic.

We can no longer see or hear anything, we are just there, in an arbitrary place at an arbitrary time, and our brains stop processing information about our surroundings or analysing data, plans, ideas, reasons for why we're here, why we are who we are, why we are at all. The world is bright, windy and cold. And we are in it.

We huddle behind a dune, my hand reaches for the cigarettes in my pocket, amazingly the lighter produces a flame, and the smoke burns in my lungs. She touches my knee when I give her a light, and I want to thank her, because for the first time in days I can feel that I actually exist.
Cold, isn't it?
Yes.

We go home.

I don't know what love is

I don't think you even know what love is, she says, running her fingernail across the fitted sheet and looking at the books on the floor beside the bed, and I look at her fingernail, then at the books, and I think, of course I don't know what love is, and I say: Of course I know what love is. Love is what we feel for each other.

She looks up at the big, grey, concrete beam on the ceiling, and I think, because we tell each other we love each other, and because we use the word love in that way, it's love, because what could love possibly be other than what is signified by the word love, and then she says, Well what is it that you feel for me?

And I say what I'm thinking, which is, I want you to be happy.

Why?

Why what?

Why do you want that?

My breathing quickens. I find the question completely unreasonable. It offends something in me. I don't know what, perhaps my idea of what the world should be like, because I believe that in a world that is good, people should be able to accept that you want them to be happy without asking why. Ungrateful creature, I think. You should be glad that I want you to be happy. Don't question it. And then I ask myself why, in fact, I want her to be happy. Perhaps it's not such a stupid question, and I then think, in that case I might as well ask myself why I want anything at all, and the answer to that question, I know, is I-don't-know and the consequence of that answer is: no. I don't want anything.

I say, Because you deserve it.

She smiles.

She smiles, but it's not the grateful, happy smile I'm expecting. It's friendly, it's maybe even loving, but there is something else in that smile, and that makes me uncomfortable, because it contains a knowledge, some truth about me and my reasons for wanting to make her happy that I cannot know, and I don't know exactly what it is that she knows, but very slowly a fear starts to take shape inside me, the fear that it's all for nothing, because my desire to make her happy isn't about her, it's about me, it's always about me. She says, You're a good person.

She turns away, and I ask myself where in my head the thing is that feels good when I say, It feels good to be with you. Where the 'I' in I love you is. And then I realise that the only thing I can say with any certainty is:

she is there. She is lying next to me in bed, close enough that I could reach out and touch her back.

And then she leaves

She's packing. She gets plastic bags out from under the sink, different colours and sizes, and shakes them out with quick, jerky movements. It's loud, so loud that it hurts my ears. She puts her shoes in the bags, then she neatly folds her jumpers and trousers and blouses, and I can hear her humming as she does all this, because she has always hummed whenever she felt like she was doing something carefully and properly and well. But then she has stopped humming, her face is harder than usual, and she is not looking at me. There's nothing more for her to see. She's got my number, she knows me, she has tried everything. And then she calmly puts on mascara before packing her numerous utensils into numerous little cases and pouches, and putting them in her suitcase, which is so big and heavy that she can barely lift it, but it doesn't matter because it's on wheels, and she puts her knee on the suitcase and closes the clasps and then she's packed and ready and the taxi is there and she kisses me on the cheek and looks at me one more time, without anger, but not without sadness and pity.

She looks at me, and I feel like a patient who has refused to take the medicine that could cure him because he doesn't like the way it's been prescribed, or the sound of the doctor's voice as she pronounced her diagnosis, or the length of the Patient Information Leaflet, and I realise that I'm not concentrating on what's happening. I know that this is an important moment in my life, a moment when something is happening that can't be undone, a big moment, a sad one, I know that, and I think that I would like to experience this moment for what it is, and that means not thinking about all sorts of other things, but being awake and honest and moved. It means feeling what's happening, here and now, and feeling what it means. But I'm not feeling that, because I'm thinking of so many different things, so I try to concentrate, I try not to have lots of different thoughts, but just the one, one single thought, and I think, For God's sake, man, just think one single thought for once, take it and hold the fuck on to it, and I concentrate, and it works, and at the precise moment when she walks out of my door for the last time and briefly turns around, I have only one single thought in my head: Patient Information Leaflet. And straight away I can tell that it's wrong, terribly, utterly wrong, and so I immediately think about something else. I ask myself something, I ask myself what I've always known I would ask myself when the time came and I let her walk out of the door. I've always known that at the precise moment that it became clear that I was letting her walk out of the door I would ask myself whether she would have let me walk out of the door too, and this is what I am asking myself, just this, and I know it's right, I know this is the question I have to ask, right now. And so I ask myself, would she have let me walk out of the door too, if I were her and she me, and I don't think she would, and then the door closes and she is gone, and there is something wrong with my eyes, probably the light, the sun is shining right in my face. I go to the window, I peer outside, and the light hurts my eyes, but I look out all the same, and I am looking in every possible direction except down, where at this very moment she is getting into a taxi and disappearing from my life, forever. I don't look, I just stare at the sky, I see houses, roofs, bridges. I see helicopters, cars, trains. I see air ducts, fire escapes, electrical towers, chimneys, smoke.

I am alone

We're sitting on big boulders by the East River, and it's raining on the abandoned sugar refinery to our left, on the cargo ships in front of us, on the postcard panorama with the commoditised skyline of this city, which right now is not really a postcard panorama because of the rain falling on it. The place is the same as ever, just as we expected, just as millions of people expect when they come every day and go home disappointed or happy because their expectations were met, and this is exactly the place they thought it would be. The sky is grey, it's raining, and I say, I'm sorry. I think about how often my nose has inhaled her scent, my hands have touched her soft skin, my ears have heard her voice without even noticing it, and I say, I'm sorry. I say, I'm sorry, and I don't know if it's to her or to the world, and I also don't know where the one ends and the other begins, and I'm not surprised when she doesn't answer, because she's already on the plane and I am alone.

I see a melting snowman and think, I'm sorry. I see a

rusty refrigerator on the side of the road and think, I'm sorry. I see a fashionably dressed couple, walking along the water's edge in silence, a family of Chinese tourists in see-through raincoats, and a black homeless guy and I think, I'm sorry. I see an orthodox Jew and think, after a respectful and dignified pause, I'm sorry. And then I think that I'm sorry for thinking I've got a right to think that I'm sorry when I see a Jew.

I'm sorry I was ever born and ever came into her life. I'm sorry that my brain does what it does. Now I'm also sorry that I've got a Y-chromosome that produces testos-terone, which means that I feel an urge to procreate that is completely at odds with modern societal norms. I'm sorry that I sat through that lecture on consciousness all those years ago just because the lecture I had actually wanted to attend was full. I'm sorry that, as a result of sitting through it, I ended up studying philosophy for six years. I'm sorry that I then made the mistake of not thinking of philosophy as a normal profession, like being a cabinet-maker, broker, greengrocer, plumber. I'm sorry I thought philosophy was somehow more important, more essential, and I'm sorry that this presumptuousness led me to work not only with my head, like a plumber installing a toilet, but also with my heart. I'm sorry I'm afraid. I'm sorry that I find all women attractive and that when I've found one to be with I still find all the others attractive as well. I'm sorry that I know this is morally wrong, because if I were stupider or smarter or braver or cooler I would just fuck them all. I'm sorry that I never say what I'm thinking. I'm sorry I lied when I said, there's nothing about you I don't like. But why would she ask me such a question in the first place? I'm sorry that people are made in such a way that, given enough time, they always find something they don't like about everything, and that I was stupid enough to believe that suppressed impulses could ever be forgotten. I'm sorry that I prefer to watch football on my own. I'm so sorry about everything.

And then I think, I'm the one who's sorry about everything. The others don't seem to be very sorry, and I sense that the only thing I'm really sorry about, the only thing that really, truly hurts, is that one, tiny, huge thing, that amorphous, invisible, omnipotent 'I'.

THEY DON'T KNOW
ANYTHING

The things out there

Are you aware of Ned Block's criticism of my idea of targetless higher-order thoughts?

The professor is sitting at his desk, I'm standing next to him, the papers and books are piled as high as my chest. He is reading an abstract I emailed him the day before, and I think, how can such a famous professor have such a tiny, cramped office, and then I say, I believe he said, how can an empty thought about nothing create consciousness?

Exactly. And what would I reply to that?

I believe you would reply that it is not consciousness itself that is caused by the targetless higher-order thought, but merely the disposition.

Exactly. So why do you suggest here that a combination of Kriegel's self-representationalism and Chalmers' panprotopsychism would offer a solution to the problem of targetless higher-order thoughts, when in fact, as you just said, they do not pose a problem at all?

He looks at me. He is sitting at his desk in his long and narrow office in this gigantic cube with no daylight or fresh air, diagonally opposite the Empire State Building, and he is looking at me very gently and indulgently, like a man who is only too happy to forgive intellectual short-comings if only one can explain where this nonsense that one has written and sent him and which he is now obliged to read and understand came from. He just wants to understand. He feels for me, no doubt about it. I just have to tell him what it was that led me to believe that a targetless higher-order thought posed a problem, and how I can be in any doubt that a thought that is not targeted at anything is still a thought, not a thought *about* anything in particular, of course, but a thought nonethe-less, a mental state, which, because of its structural force, has the power to generate the disposition of conscious-ness. I can see his gentle, old eyes, his sagging jowls, and I say, Because I do have trouble conceiving of a thought without any content whatsoever. I consider thoughts to be functional structures of brain activity, and how can a thought without content have a function?

He looks at me. He takes a breath. He looks at me.

The thought's function, he says, and his voice sounds more high-pitched than before, much more high-pitched, as if he were speaking to a cute child, Is not to have any function.

He is still looking at me, and then I look at the wall opposite the door, at the end of this long and narrow office, and I see that it is painted yellow, and that the paint is presumably part-acrylic, and that the wall was probably machine-rendered since it's much too smooth to have been done by hand, and the building is much too big for that anyway. I look at the wall as if it were a window.

I see.

He takes a breath. I don't know what he's looking at. I'm looking at the wall.
Are you happy here in New York?
Yes.
What do you do?
What do I do?
I look back at him.
When you're not working on this.
He nods his head in the direction of my abstract, which is now lying on his desk.
I go for walks. I listen to music. (I lie.)
Do you see people?
Yes, sometimes.
Have you met some of the other students?
Yes.
Do you go out for beer?
He smiles. I smile back. We both know that the Germans like beer, just like the Americans and the Czechs, and the Laotians, and the Thais, and the French, and the Swiss,

and probably all non-Muslim nationalities on the planet, but I try to smile as if he's figured me out, because I want him to think he's figured me out, and I want him to be pleased with himself.

Yes, we do.

He is pleased.

Excellent. Always remember: you are in New York. Go out. Meet people. Have fun. Don't stay in too much. Don't work too much. You can do that when you are back in Germany.

You are right, Professor. Thank you very much.

We don't shake hands. We did that the first time we met, and probably we will again the last time, so instead I merely nod and sidle out of the tiny crack between the desk and the wall. He turns back to his work, I walk out of the open door and step into the fluorescent light of the corridor, and I think, New York is the only place where I can really sit in a room and stare out of the window and think, Out there is New York.

Solid ground

Back at home, I open an email the professor sent me after I left his office: Read some of the basics again – it's always good to build an argument on solid ground. So I read an article about whether it's possible for us to know what it's like to be a bat, but all the while, I am imagining her sitting in an aluminium tube as it glides through the blackness over the Atlantic Ocean, through a storm front. Flashes of lightning outside the double-layered windows illuminate eye masks and noses, closed eyes and open mouths, saliva running over lips. Here and there a reading light shines on a belly that rises and falls with feigned equanimity, honest fear.

Then I read an article about a hypothetical super-scientist called Mary, who was born and grew up in a black-and-white room and who has learned all the physical facts about the world via black-and-white TV screens, and it's not clear whether she would learn anything when she saw a red rose for the first time.

As I read, I am imagining her entering her kitchen with

the dark brown wood floor and the orange cupboards, holding the kettle under the running tap, putting it back on its base and turning it on and then setting about chopping ginger: chop, chop, chop, chop, chop.

I read an article about hypothetical beings who are physically identical to us in every way and whose behaviour is indistinguishable from our own, but who are characterised by total interior darkness, people with absolutely no conscious experience, zombies.

I'm imagining her pouring boiling water on pieces of ginger in a thick-walled glass, the pleasantly acrid smell rising up into her nose so she goes, Mmmh.

I read an article about a brain in a vat connected to a computer that makes it believe it is a human living his life, and I'm imagining her sitting down on the sofa with her ginger tea, taking off her shoes, tucking up her legs and, with her free hand, covering them with a blanket.

I read an article about an experiment that would recreate the human brain using the entire population of China, one person per synapse, and I'm imagining her turning on the TV, which is showing a music video by Alicia Keys and Jay-Z, *Empire State of Mind*. I imagine how the image becomes blurry because her eyes are growing moist, but she doesn't cry, she would rather sing, and so she sings along at the top of her voice, sings against the tears and disappointment and the fact that she's singing her favourite song at home, and not where it was written and with the man she would once have wanted to sing it for, and she holds the ginger tea up close to her face and sings, into the tea, into the empty living room, and out into our dark, cold, meaningless hometown.

I stop reading. The Empire State Building is shining blue.

I imagine her plaiting her hair. She is sitting up straight. She is looking intently in the mirror. She is humming, as her fingers skilfully weave the strands together. I imagine the air in the bathroom, she showered maybe fifteen minutes ago, the mirror is no longer steamed up, but the air is still warmer than in the corridor or in the living room. She looks at her hair as it forms a plait, strand by strand. Slowly but surely, she knows that the plait will be perfect and that with it she will be beautiful.

I imagine her making earrings. She takes alabaster pearls, pieces of varnished ebony and splinters of mother of pearl, spears them with a sharp needle and strings them along a nylon cord that is attached to an ear stud. After having strung each individual object, she holds the provisional earring up and inspects it from various angles, then she holds it up to her ear and takes the little hand mirror lying next to her on the bed where she is sitting cross-legged, and then she looks at herself and the earring for a while. Finally, she places it back on the white cloth in front of her, where the pieces of wood and precious stones and feathers are laid out, and she removes whatever is too much and adds whatever is missing.

I imagine her getting dressed and leaving the house. I imagine the sound of her shoes on the pavement, the soft jangle of her earrings and bracelets, her smell. I imagine her waiting until she's on the street before calling her friends and telling them what's happened. I imagine how they'll understand; they'll say they're on their way, they'll hurry, and not long after they'll be sitting at a bar in Glockenbach. They'll skip the white wine spritzers and go straight to gin and tonics. I imagine them at a club, P1, Paradiso, Erste Liga. I imagine her dancing. I imagine how she looks when she dances. I imagine how lots of people are watching her dance.

I think about how people are seventy-two per cent water. I think about how we live on a ball travelling at one-hundred-and-seven-thousand-two-hundred-and-eight kilometres an hour around the sun. I imagine a cat suspended between life and death. I imagine the number pi. I imagine a square circle. I imagine her sleeping with someone else.

I turn out the lights

They don't know anything. They don't look at me any differently when I come into the building, when I pass the neoclassical columns on either side of the entrance, when I cross the lobby with the security guards, the burgundy tapestries, the brass doorknobs and the marble floor. Is this a university or a casino? They think, if they think anything, he's on his way to give a lecture, but most likely they don't think anything at all. I show them my pass, they nod, if that, they don't say, No, you can't come in here, never again. They don't say any of those things, not yet.

Maybe, when I pass familiar faces in the foyer or the lift or the corridor, I notice the edges of a few mouths, or chins, or pairs of eyebrows, are raised. But I can still simply walk into the room with the number I memorised when they gave me the date and time: 7112. The room is pretty full. There are about fifty people here.

The professor whose guest I still am still introduces me,

he still says kind things about me and my project and the great distance I've travelled from Germany to be here today in this room, with them, to tell them what I think. They are still listening.

They are looking at me. They are looking at me with their many eyes, all different and yet all the same: sceptical. They are looking at me. I am not looking at them. They are staring at me. I scan the assembled crowd, one after the other, third from the left, second from the back, fourth from the right in the front, and then I concentrate on the solitary unused socket in the wall at the rear, right-hand corner of the room. The room is wider than it is long. That's not a bad thing. Before me there is a small crowd of people, not an impersonal, amorphous mass, but rather just this strip of open eyes, five, six rows deep, ten pairs wide. The heads in which the eyes are imbedded are held high, you might describe the attitude as proud: yes, we are here to listen to you, and, yes, we are educated enough to be here to listen to you, and, yes, we are educated and focused and above all quick enough to notice if you make a mistake, sonny. If what you say is bullshit, we'll know it before you do, and then we'll make sure you know it. We'll raise our hands, and you will know you're about to get your ass kicked, and we will wait for you to call on us, politely, one at a time, so that we can mop the floor with you, as dictated by the rules and decorum and by your manners, if you have any, and we're sure you do, otherwise you wouldn't be here, this is the City University of New York, bitch, and we're here to do philosophy, so you'd better have some arguments. Welcome!

Have I got arguments? Let me tell you. I'm going to tell you all in a moment. I'm going to explain to you exactly what consciousness is. After all, I've been preparing for this for a long time. So I look at the first slide of my PowerPoint presentation, and it has words on it like: metarepresentation, qualia, intrinsicalism. And suddenly they seem so strange to me. Because all I really want to say is the obvious, what everyone knows, namely that if, while doing something, you at the same time think about the fact that you are doing it, you will do it less well, because you are using part of the resources you need for doing or thinking to think: what am I doing?

I can see your blue, green, brown eyes, your yellow, white, black skin, I can see your hair, if you still have any, I can see whether you spent any time in front of the mirror thinking about your hair, and I can see whether they were good thoughts or bad. I can see your clothes, T-shirt, hoodie, leather dress, designer shirt and boots and ortho-paedic sandals for indoors, and hiking boots, trainers and high heels with rubber soles because of the rain, I can see the colour of the wall behind you and the pigments in the carpet, the aluminium of the tables and chairs and the dark imitation wood in between, and I can see the dust particles dancing in the light of the projector.

I can see the water bottle on the lectern next to my laptop and the glass next to it, and the glass is so transparent and clean, the bottle too, and the water most of all, and then I look back at the faces in front of me and at the bodies and at the chairs on which the bodies are sitting and at the floor on which the chairs are standing, and here and there I can see a pair of feet, and I can see the tables and walls and air vents in the ceiling and the fluorescent lights, and I can see the shadows cast by the bodies in the fluorescent light and the shadows are always different because there are many fluorescent lights and many bodies and many different angles between the bodies and the lights, and I can see that it's all so much and so different, and then I look back at the water bottle.

I pour some water into the glass. Someone clears their throat. I take the glass, raise it up to my mouth, and I don't raise my eyes because I know that no matter how I look at what's in front of me, it will not change, it will always be uneven, colourful, and profuse, the water tastes clear and clean.

Excuse me? I think we are all curious to hear your talk. Would you like to begin?

I take another sip of water. I can feel the cold of the liquid, or rather its non-heat, I can see its non-colour, apprehend its non-form. I can feel something descending and spreading inside me, a substance that comes from somewhere out there, from condensed drops inside clouds, or from layers of rock inside the earth, or from rivers winding across plains or lakes high up in the mountains. I can feel something that was 'not-I' becoming 'I', becoming part of 'me', somewhere deep inside me this process is taking place, in the dark, and the water takes on my temperature, my colour, my form.

It becomes 'I'. And the people are becoming restless. And I am not looking at them. I can see the dust particles in front of the projector lamp. And suddenly I understand. I understand how arrogant it is to assume that a brain is something better than these circling particles of dust, and I think that the structure of my brain is just slightly more complex than that of these dust particles, namely in the sense that it can wonder why it is constructed in such a way that it can wonder why it is constructed in such a way, and so on.

And suddenly I know that each part of my brain in

isolation is just as complex and just as boring, just as meaningless and just as beautiful as these dust particles in the light of the projector, and so I relax, let go, decide that for today I will leave my brain in peace. Take it easy, brain, you're OK, look at the dust particles, aren't they beautiful?

And suddenly all other questions seem meaningless, and they quietly and carefully evaporate, and in my head there is nothing but happiness about the clear water in the dark inside me and the dust particles in front of me in the light, and I know they probably don't know that they're particles of dust, but that doesn't matter, they are there and they are beautiful, they are particles of dust.

And the people in the room are getting louder and louder, and they say, This is ridiculous, and they start getting up and packing their things, and out of the corner of my eye I can see them gesticulating at me and shaking their heads and two of them are already heading for the exit and suddenly I'm even more relaxed, even freer, even more content. I know I haven't said a word because I have finally understood that words can't help you understand what consciousness is. Words are the death of conscious- ness, of experience, and thus of life. It's the things that matter, only the things, and in each thing there is a tiny consciousness, a hundred times, a million times smaller and truer and more genuine than this complex, self-reflexive consciousness of ours, yours and mine. We are not the world, the world is the things out there.

On my way out, I turn out the lights.

HERE I AM

The windows are black

I step outside. I put one foot in front of the other, I move in a specific direction towards a specific destination, I know where I am going, but I don't need to articulate it, because my destination surrounds my body. I am caught in its pull, forward, onward, and my movement towards this destination is as elementary and all-consuming and impersonal as the relationship between my lungs and the oxygen that surrounds the earth, ready to be inhaled.

I walk. I stop. A car. I walk on. I cross a street, Kent and North 3rd, and a neural pattern independent of the part of my brain that constitutes my persona and its experience devises a potential route: left on Metropolitan, right on Wythe, left on North 1st, right on Berry, left on Grand, right on Bedford, left on South 1st, right on Driggs, left on South 2nd, right on Roebling, left on South 3rd, right on Havemeyer, left on South 4th, right on Marcy, Marcy, Marcy, Marcy. I follow it.

I see: a Jewish supermarket, a Jewish hat shop, a Jewish

second-hand shop, a Jewish hardware store, a Jewish pharmacy, a Jewish post office, a Jewish butcher's and delicatessen, a florist's which may or may not be Jewish, at least the sign isn't in Hebrew script, a clothing shop, likewise without any indication of the owners' religion, as well as: a diner, a steakhouse, the car park in front of the steakhouse, the parking attendant for the steakhouse, the bus-turning circle, buses, the bridge access ramp, the bridge, the greengrocers under the bridge, the second-hand shops under the bridge, the electronics shops under the bridge, the sports-shoe shops under the bridge, and then: the stairs.

One after the other, my feet touch each individual step, next to the steps there is a grate to prevent you from falling down onto the street in front of the buses, cars, fire engines, lorries, taxis and police cars. I reach the platform and look at the view: façades and roofs, façades and roofs, until this view is interrupted by the inevitable arrival of the subway train.

The subway train is clean and silver, the doors of the train shine, the train is hot, even though here it is above ground. The doors open, I get on, see people of various colours and shapes, variously dressed, with various destinations. The doors close, the train, which runs above ground here, starts moving. It moves slowly, the ascent onto the bridge, the noise, just noise for now and the view from the bridge of the water. Above the bridge: other bridges, on them other trains, in them other people, the opposite shore, the tunnel, the noise, the noise of the destruction of space, its violent separation into here and there. The windows are black.

Or a mirror, depending on one's depth of field. Images of bodies and clothes and handrails and emergency brakes move together in this specific section of the solar system, surrounded by noise, carrying us past stations I don't get off at, brief interruptions in the blackness on the way to a specific light.

I see the floor of the carriage. From the perspective of the carriage it is not moving, from an absolute perspective, it is, and over a certain period of time it picks up speed, which can be calculated based on various basic properties of the universe such as impetus, mass, inertia, gravity. I am standing firmly on the floor of this subway train, which is accelerating along a clearly defined trajectory towards a clearly defined goal, my hand is grasping an iron bar upon which there are microbes that pose no threat to my immune system. I shift my weight from one foot to the other based on signals from my muscles and from an organ in my auditory canal, the floor is moving and the system in my ears tells those muscles which have to contract to contract, so that I keep my balance on this floor which is moving, on tracks laid down on a planet that is also moving, and then the train stops moving, and I get off.

I step out onto the street. I cross it. I get to the other side. Houses everywhere, they are made of wood, stone and steel, of cement, plaster and glass. I walk past them, and then I stop in front of a building, right in front of the opening in the middle, one metre wide, two metres tall, and above the opening there is a sign, and I turn the body that is me ninety degrees to the right, towards the opening, and in the opening it is dark, almost black, and I walk through the opening and then I am inside.

I can feel my heart beating

I am standing in a darkened room. My feet are on the floor. The floor is touching walls on which things are hanging, things which stand out from the wall, materially, chromatically, and functionally. Someone is standing next to me, and next to him and in front of and behind us are more people. No one has determined the exact number of people here, but there are a lot. The bodies of those standing here are touching, and their voices and gazes overlap. Together they have been able to raise the room temperature to a degree that each of them individually would describe as unbearable.

I notice that the noise level rises the moment the television screen above the bar shows a ball lying on a table in front of a field at the end of a tunnel, and next to the ball stands a trophy, and it's not that people are talking more or talking faster than before, they're just talking louder, in the room in which I am standing, and in other rooms in which I am not, on the opposite side of the street, the city, the continent, the ocean.

An unimaginable number of pairs of eyes are perceiving an unimaginable number of reproductions at different resolutions of an image of a ball next to a trophy, the volume on the television has to be turned up because the chatter in front of the televisions has grown louder because the voices of the television commentators have grown louder because the chatter in the ten-storey oval around the field where the ball is lying on a table next to a trophy has grown louder.

They are talking about the game two days ago, or the one five days ago, or about politics, about countries where people are dying to prevent other people from dying, and they are complaining about the Muslims if they're not Muslims themselves, or about the Christians if they're not Christians themselves, or about religion, stupidity, backwardness and self-inflicted poverty. They are also talking about the new song by so-and-so, such-and-such a brand of clothing, about their incomes, tax law, shares, returns and criminal banks, about pets, kids, schools and juvenile delinquency, about foreigners, cars, breasts, and beer.

Their voices take on a sharp, important air, even though they know that what they're talking about is banal, or because they know it. The longer the conversation goes on, the clearer it becomes that it doesn't matter what they are saying, but that they are here, now, saying it, just before it starts, and the conversations of billions of people, each of whom on average says three words per second, in one-hundred-and-ninety-four countries spread over every time and climate zone, are just sound waves, randomly produced by vocal cords and shaped by mouths, spreading through nitrogen, carbon dioxide and oxygen, they have no function besides traversing the timespan it takes for them to fade away, and they are growing harder, more precise, shorter, louder, clearer, more monotonous, brighter, more alert, the words are waiting for something that has nothing whatsoever to do with what their sound would indicate, and the people uttering these words know it, and they keep talking, never stop talking, and the camera pans away from the ball on the table next to the trophy, across the green towards the wall of people on the other side and then back to the ball and the table and then further into the dark corridor behind it. In the tunnel there is movement.

I can see that there is movement in the tunnel and I sense a gentle tug at the base of my spine, just a gentle one, thankfully. I've taken half an ibuprofen, I think it'll be all right, partly because of the ibuprofen and partly because of the player who will be wearing the number 7 when he emerges from the tunnel, in which right now there is movement. You can't yet tell what it is, perhaps it's the player wearing the number 7. I shift my weight to the leg that is stronger at this particular moment, I take a sip of beer, I move my back away from the bar, I rest my right elbow on the bar, I take another sip of beer, I turn ninety degrees, I lean back on the bar, I put down my glass. For a while I stand here like this, and I see something moving in the tunnel, it is wearing a specific colour, and I don't yet know which one, but I can see that it is a colour, definitely, and I hear the voices around me growing louder and the temperature hotter and the elbows harder and the bellies even softer and the buttocks more determined, and I push away from the bar and take a step to the side, dodging a foot on the floor, stepping on another foot, someone else steps on mine, and I say, Scuse me, wanker.

I say wanker when I see that the first player to come out of the tunnel is wearing a particular colour. I say *olé*. I don't say anything. I just sip my beer, and I confidently grab the side of the woman standing next to me, and I am staring at her arse and into her cleavage. I am and I'm not. I am looking only at that dark tunnel, at the men stepping out of it into the light and into the noise of the billions. Here they come.

I take a sip of beer. Here they come. I'm a tax account-ant. Here they come. I give people advice when they have questions about their tax returns, I'm good at my job, thankfully, that's why I can stand here and order beer and pay for it and drink it. They're coming out in the right and in the wrong colours, and they're running out onto the pitch, and I take a sip of beer. I take a sip of beer, I'm a night watchman, and they're still running out onto the pitch and some of them are waving at me, my job is to keep an eye on objects that need protecting, I provide this protection and after a trial period, I will get a gun, a Heckler & Koch 9 millimetre, and I hope I won't have to shoot anyone in the face with it. I'm a peace-loving person. Some of the players are shaking hands despite the fact that they are wearing different colours. If someone tries to take one of the objects that I am charged with protecting, boom. I take a sip of beer. They are running nimbly and powerfully to the edge of the field in that ten-storey oval. I'm a plumber, a mechanic, a mechatronic engineer. They're jumping up and down, limbering up their muscles. I mend burst pipes. They're adjusting their socks and shin guards. I prevent petrol pumps from exploding. They're standing together for the team portrait. I make sure brakes brake, I am in charge of transmissions and engines and ball bearings that regulate light and dark. I'm an investment banker. I'm unemployed. I'm a teacher, I'm a journalist, I'm an insurance broker, and I do what I do because I can. There they are. I take a sip of beer.

I have hair. I have skin. I have a heart. I have a name. I beat a man up this morning. I got a woman pregnant last night. I've got toothache. I'm wearing odd socks. I would never admit that I say my prayers before bed. I sometimes look out of the window. I know seven different types of flowers. I have a mother. I have a garden with a path through a meadow, a path made of clean, white stones. Yesterday, at the end of my shift at the maternity ward, I threw away a bagful of placentas. I slept next to a dumpster, and with my cheek I could feel the tiny irregularities in the tarmac. I gave a beggar fifty cents yesterday, and when he saw that was all that I had, he gave me a quarter back, and I said thank you. I once pissed on a cat, I was drunk, it was pretty funny. I've faked an orgasm. I didn't notice. At my confirmation I thought about shit, about light brown, soft shit, not in a bowl or on some surface or other, but divorced from the world, just shit in itself. I have constructed a design for my life that achieves the perfect balance between money, sport, food, love, and sleep. I've got a jumper that's a little faded and a little too short, but it keeps me warm all the same, so I still wear it, sometimes it's still really quite cold out, even though it's already April.

There they are. They are standing on a field, some of them wearing one colour, the others another, and the people all around me have stopped making the effort of articulating the sounds coming out of their mouths and noses. Now we are shouting.

They are running onto the pitch. We are shouting. They

look determined, young, and brave. We are shouting, and they are still pretending that the ball, which right now is being placed on the white dot in the middle of all that green, surrounded by walls forested with people, by cameras, by the world, doesn't really matter. We are shouting. They raise their faces to those forest walls, hold them up to the cameras and the world, and they are ready and willing to be filled up with all our hopes, our rage, our hatred. They will carry it all for us, and they will take it with them when they attack our enemies. We are shouting.

Now I am grabbing the cold metal railing separating the stands from the pitch. Now I am putting the remote control on the end table. Now I am touching the grass, now I am ripping up a few blades, now I am rubbing them between my fingers, now I am crossing myself. I can feel my heart beating. I nod to the others. Now all I see is the ball.